Also by Vincent Wilde

The Combat Zone: A Cody Harper Novel, Book One

AN
ABSENT
GOD

AN
ABSENT
GOD

A CODY HARPER NOVEL

VINCENT WILDE

CLEIS
PRESS

Published in the United States by Cleis Press, an imprint of Start Midnight, LLC, 101 Hudson Street, Thirty-Seventh Floor, Suite 3705, Jersey City, NJ 07302.

Printed in the United States.
Cover design: Scott Idleman/Blink
Cover photograph: iStock
Text design: Frank Wiedemann

First Edition.
10 9 8 7 6 5 4 3 2 1

Trade ISBN: 978-1-62778-212-8
Ebook ISBN: 978-1-62778-213-5

To Michael—
for making life worth living.

CHAPTER
ONE

NEW YORK CITY—1996

BILL CLINTON HAD WON THE PRESIDENTIAL
election. To say I was underwhelmed would be an understatement. The news came in over the television networks as I drank
an espresso at a Greenwich Village coffee shop. Bob Dole and
Ross Perot had failed to unseat Clinton and I wanted the whole
election process to be over. A few patrons stood, lifted their coffee
cups high, and applauded. I lit a cigarette, took another sip, and
returned to a book of poetry by J. D. McClatchy.

As far as I was concerned, the whole Reverend Rodney Jessup
affair had ended any faint love affair I had with politics. Like a
stumbling racehorse, Jessup hardly made it out of the gate. He was
disgraced—as washed up as the plastic bottles that littered the
Hudson. The preacher turned presidential candidate made his exit
sometime in April when he withdrew his candidacy. *That's what a
sex scandal will do to a pretender to the throne.* John Dresser, my
old friend and Stephen Cross's boyfriend, had precipitated Jessup's

fall after I found Stephen dead, along with two other victims of the Combat Zone Killer, hanging on a cross. All it took was the Reverend's recovered thumbprint and the name of a New York City porn theater written on one of his old business cards. The fact that Stephen's former New Haven address was scrawled on the card didn't hurt either. Jessup was kaput, gone bye-bye, a brief, sputtering comet in the world of presidential politics.

He was done and so was I.

I closed my book, still salivating over McClatchy's beautiful lines, dropped a few bucks as a tip on the table, zipped up my leather jacket, and headed for the street. The evening was breezy and cool, but not bone-chilling. I had walked uptown in a lot worse weather. It was my night off from my employment as a dishwasher at Han's Chinese, a job I'd held for more than a year. Mr. Han was a small Cantonese man with shining black hair and equally glittering eyes. No fool he. He knew he was getting a good deal at my hourly rate, but I often surprised myself at how much I enjoyed my new vocation. I had learned a smattering of Cantonese and had been welcomed into an extended family of sons, daughters, relatives, and aging grandparents. Besides, I liked sticking my hands in soapy dishwater. Sometimes the itch to apply for a bodyguard's license or to leave New York rose up like ants crawling under my skin, and when it did, those warm, comfy suds calmed me down. There'd be a lot less murders in the world if everyone was required to stick their hands in hot water for eight hours a day.

I looked eastward down Thirty-Fourth. The Empire State Building shone back, its top tiers swathed in stratified layers of red, white, and blue lights. This, I presumed, was in celebration of our wonderful electoral process—a system I had never participated in. I was much more about action than process. The lights would blink out at some point and everyone would get back to business as usual now that the election had ended.

After Stephen disappeared, I moved into a basement apartment near Forty-Seventh and Tenth Avenue. I had been tempted to leave a couple of times when the cockroaches decided to eat off my plate, or when I felt too sun deprived, but the rent was cheap and I had come to think of it as my own little nest. I know it's gross to say, but I thought of it like a rat's burrow. God knows there are enough rats in New York City without my contribution. But I liked the close comfort my nest provided. I had dropped out of sight after Stephen's disappearance, as much for safety's sake as out of grief over my unrequited love for Stephen Cross. I didn't want anyone to find me while I shed a bad pile of memories—including John Dresser; other Boston friends like Win Hart and Ophelia Cox who had slipped from my mind; Rodney Jessup, or his wife Carol, or any of his crew, such as Janice Carpenter, his public relations pit bull. And no one had.

Until now.

A late-model black Mercedes idled one space down from my door. Some gentrification had sprouted in Hell's Kitchen now that Mayor Giuliani was cleaning up Forty-Second Street; however, a luxury sedan in my neighborhood was an oddity. I didn't routinely carry heat these days, unless you considered dishpan hands a dangerous weapon, and the sight of the car gave me the creeps. For the first time in a year, I felt exposed and naked. Something about the black vehicle sent a shiver up my spine—call it my gift of prophecy revealed to me by a Boston fortune-teller, or the fact that I had read about Rodney Jessup's Mercedes in Stephen's diary.

I stopped about half a block away and studied the car. No exhaust poured out, but that didn't mean anything. The car could have been idling long enough to mask any fumes dispersing into the chilly air. Its windows were dark and tinted, and anyone who might have been in the car was hidden behind the smoked glass.

I stood for a few more minutes before lighting another cigarette. When my lighter flared, the driver's-side window slid down about a third of the way. Reason number 101 for not smoking: it gives away your cover. I caught sight of something—a pair of eyes peering past the open glass. The window glided silently up and the brief show was over.

I'd had enough paranoia. I didn't think anyone would shoot me on the street, but knowing my history of small-time drug dealing, hustling, and to-die-for drag, anything could happen. I threw caution to the wind and walked down the block, away from the Mercedes, so I could circle behind the car to my apartment. The tag was hard to read, but as I got closer I saw it wasn't from New York. It had Virginia plates.

My heart thumped in my chest and the back of my neck burned like I had been out in the sun too long.

I stayed on the sidewalk, close to the doorways in case I needed to duck inside for cover. When I was parallel to the car, the passenger-side window hissed down, revealing a pair of jeaned legs under the steering column, hands on the wheel, and a man in the passenger seat who looked familiar. I picked up my pace.

"Mr. Harper?" a voice called out.

I recognized the Southern lilt, the slight drawl that spun like silk over my name. I'd last heard that voice in a church more than a year ago in Manchester, New Hampshire.

The passenger leaned toward the window and a face came into view—the thin white face of the Reverend Rodney Jessup.

"Cody . . . I need to talk to you," he said. "It's important."

I wasn't sure what to say, but I sputtered, "The election's over, Reverend. You lost."

He smiled and said, "For some people that's not enough. Do you mind if *we* come in?"

The question came out in a boozy slur and I smelled scotch on his breath, his drink of choice. But, still, he looked calm enough under the half shadows of the streetlamp. The driver hadn't moved and I didn't see a weapon.

"Who's we, and why?"

"My bodyguard. I think you'd like him, but, more to the point, you're good at finding people. You managed to track down Stephen Cross. I need you to help me find someone."

I threw my cigarette in the gutter and stepped toward the window. I bent down and looked in. To the observer on the street, it might look as if Rodney Jessup was trying to pay me for sex. I had been in this position many times before. I glanced over at the driver. Holy guacamole. He was a dish, fully baked, and good looking. Hispanic, with eyes so dark I could barely see them in the dim light. I had no trouble seeing his muscles, however. My gaydar punched in at full tilt. Still, I wasn't used to aiding and abetting the enemy.

"You've got balls, Rodney. Coming to me for help after you betrayed Stephen." A red heat rushed into my face. Anger I hadn't experienced since Stephen's death boiled up again—and not in a good way. A few loose pieces of broken sidewalk lay nearby, and I thought about how easy it would be to hurl them through Rodney Jessup's windshield.

"You know I didn't kill him."

"No, you obsequious son of a bitch, but your silence and subterfuge contributed to his death. In my book, you're as guilty as Aryan America and even the Combat Zone Killer himself."

Rodney sighed and leaned against the door. I thought he might break out in one of those old-time religion hymns or maybe start praying for me. The last thing I wanted was a prayer from Rodney Jessup, and I was prepared to make sure that didn't happen. I wrapped both hands over the window casing and squeezed. I imagined them around Rodney's throat.

"I know . . . and I've lost other people dear to me because of my sins."

"Cut the crap, Rodney. You ain't on the pulpit. A sob story won't cut it with me."

He banged his fists on the leather-padded dash and then turned to me. His eyes sparkled in the light of the streetlamp. "What the hell do you want? My family is in danger—Carol and the children. You know the players from the Combat Zone murders better than anyone."

His voice broke and he swiped at tears.

His pain was somewhat touching, but I questioned the sincerity of his plea. Why me? Why not get a private investigator, or just contact the local cops in good ole Virginee? It didn't make sense.

"Sorry, Rodney. You'll forgive me if I don't open up my insect-infested apartment to you. Who knows? You might be allergic to Raid, and I really don't want to hear jokes down the road about how you slummed it one night with a drag queen in Hell's Kitchen." And just to stab the ice pick in the heart, I added, "And, besides, you might drop a business card."

The booze made him oblivious to my venom. "I just want to talk. I only need fifteen minutes of your time."

"Maybe fifteen minutes with your driver. But you—not interested." I let go of the car and stood up, prepared to walk away.

I couldn't see his face, but he called out after me, "There's a lot of money in it for you. Say, half-a-million dollars."

Stephen had a bounty on his head of a half-mil before he was murdered by the Combat Zone Killer.

I turned back to the car, leaned in, and got in Rodney's face. "You really are a no good motherfucker."

Close up, he looked creased and spent, but his voice was calm and steady when he replied, "I need you for this job. I'll even pay for you to get a bodyguard license." He pulled a card out of the breast pocket of his white oxford shirt. "Call me when you're ready."

If nothing else, I wanted the card as evidence, so I took it and walked away.

About halfway to my door I shouted back, "How did you find me?"

"The phone book," he said as the window rose.

"My number's unlisted."

The window closed and the Mercedes pulled out from the curb, turned right at the corner, and sped away uptown in a flash of black and red.

I put the key in my door. *Damn, there goes the neighborhood.*

CHAPTER TWO

MY RUN-IN WITH RODNEY THREW ME INTO A
tailspin and sent my paranoia meter soaring. When I switched
on the apartment lights, I didn't know who would be waiting for
me: a hit man, a thug Jessup had hired to rough me up—or worse
yet, if Jessup knew my address, what was to stop Aryan America
from finding me?

My apartment was not as bad as I had made it out to be to
Jessup. I had my reasons for telling him it was infested—I didn't
want to play host to a man I loathed for his connections—at least
in my mind—to the Combat Zone Killer. I had fixed it up in the
year I had been there—cleaned like a banshee and dragged in some
furniture that I had found on the street. Clutter was one of my
weaknesses, but I didn't like to spend much time indoors if I could
help it. The rooms were dark most of the year and I needed light
to preserve my sanity. My predilection for going through junk had
kicked in early in my occupancy at Forty-Seventh and Tenth. I
started to gather books and records again, but I soon put the kibosh
on my collecting habit. There was no room. Unlike my rather airy

digs in Boston, my New York apartment was close and confined, and I really didn't want to live in a claustrophobic firetrap.

My job at Han's Chinese allowed me certain luxuries I'd never had. By luxuries, I meant things most people took for granted: new sheets, a telephone, a cheap gym membership, an occasional dinner out. I'd even gotten a New York driver's license, although I didn't own a car. I also tried meeting people again. That was the hardest task of my new life because I was a loner by nature and distrustful of all the shit people tried to pull. My naturally cynical side had saved my life many a time, and I always appreciated its value. Okay, so I went to a gay bar now and then. I still didn't drink or do drugs—I had been sober long before I came to New York. My alcoholism ended years ago, so it was hard to strike up a conversation in an environment where everyone else was three sheets to the wind. The leather community had embraced me from the beginning and I was drawn to it in New York. I'd reassessed the sex life I'd lost over the past year while dealing with the Combat Zone murders. The strictly defined roles of leather added order to my sex life, but so far it had been confined to a few titillating role-plays, nothing more. I longed for the role-play of master and slave. Many a subservient had found pleasure under me while I wielded the lash.

I looked around the living room, peered into my tiny bedroom, and then plopped on the couch. My nerves jangled and I pulled my cigarettes out of my jacket pocket. I was just about to light up when the phone rang. I jumped up and swore because, like my address, my phone number wasn't listed in the phone book. Bad news for sure. I picked up the receiver and held it to my ear without saying a word.

"Hello . . . hello?" The voice sounded familiar but I didn't immediately recognize it. I was about to hang up when the man said, "Sorry, wrong number."

"Who is this?" I asked.

"Des?"

I knew the caller's identity immediately after he said my name in that chatty, girlfriend kind of way. None other than Win Hart, a good friend of Stephen Cross's boyfriend, John Dresser. Win had worked as a trainer at the Body Club with John when everything was still nicey-nice in Boston.

"What's up, Win?"

He sighed. "Girl, am I glad I found you. It's been a long time. John gave me your number."

"I guess it's everyone's night to find me. Good news comes in bunches." Not that I didn't want to talk to Win, but he wasn't my closest friend, and during the investigation that followed Stephen's disappearance, he thought I'd killed a trick. That false impression didn't exactly make us bosom buddies.

Win wanted to catch up and I told him as much about my life after Stephen as I cared to. I didn't mention seeing Rodney Jessup and didn't have much else to tell. My life had been pretty pedestrian, carving out a meager existence in New York. I'm sure Win thought I was out fighting crime on every front like some comic book superhero, or maybe he thought I was turning tricks and doing drag at one of the local clubs. Hell, the television with rabbit ears I'd picked up off the street barely got one channel. I couldn't even talk intelligently about *The X-Files*. My life was boring, with a capital *B*.

"John's living in Florida now," he said.

I knew John had moved to Pensacola to live with his sister for a while, but we had lost track of each other.

"He's in Fort Lauderdale," Win continued. "He seems to like it. I don't know what he sees in Florida. Way too many old people, and it's too damn hot! You couldn't drag me there unless I was a vegetable in a wheelchair. I like the seasons. You need spring, summer, fall, and winter fashions. Besides, I got the job as assistant manager of the Body Club after John left."

"I guess he'd had enough of the cold," I said, and thought the conversation must blessedly be near the end.

But Win surprised me.

"There's something I need to tell you," he said, and paused, building on his innate flair for drama. "It's about Ophelia Cox."

That got my attention. Ophelia was the black drag goddess who taught me everything I knew about the art and then some. She was sleek, sophisticated, and as classy as they came. She also turned tricks. The last time I saw Ophelia, she was standing outside the Déjà Vu in Boston before the whole Stephen Cross affair exploded.

"I know you know Ophelia. She's a good woman . . . but she's had a tough time lately. She has AIDS."

My heart sank. "I'm sorry."

"Well, it's not exactly a death sentence anymore, but I think Ophelia could use a friend. And I know you knew her in Boston. She's living in New York now and I have her address and phone number if you'd like it."

I took Ophelia's information from Win and we hung up with a promise to keep in touch. That seemed more likely now that Ophelia's illness was unfolding.

I put the phone back on the table, switched on all the lights in my apartment, and picked up a book to read. I settled again on the couch, but found I was fidgeting with the pages and not concentrating on anything but being alone. I was sorry for Ophelia's illness, but I wondered if I wasn't sorry for myself as well. The chill of loneliness crept over me. Ophelia and I had slept together a few times but eventually broke off our sexual relationship. I was a bit more primal than she was. She was like a black cat, sexy and silky, but just as likely to wander off for her next conquest with a detached "had you" look in her eyes. I liked her a lot and I could have fallen, but I didn't. Everything she taught me about drag enriched my life. I owed it to her to at least be a friend. I looked at the address. It was on the Lower East Side, in a less than stellar neighborhood. I decided I would make the trip to her apartment the next afternoon before work.

I woke up late the next day and gave Ophelia a call. The phone rang six times before kicking into the answering machine. I couldn't tell if the voice was hers, so I didn't leave a message. Everyone, including Stephen, had urged me to get a machine when I lived in Boston. I still couldn't stand the stupid things. Someday, when I'd earned enough money for extended psychotherapy, I would explore my phobia about answering machines. For the moment, I chalked it up to my longtime fear of commitment—receiving a message meant I had to call someone back. Ugh.

My shift at Han's started at three p.m., so I had a few hours. I decided to hop on the train and take the forty-five-minute journey to Ophelia's apartment. Maybe I'd be lucky enough to find her at home. The day was pleasant enough for November. The late fall sun poured through the caverns created by Midtown's high-rise buildings; a few puffy clouds streaked across the sky, weaving between glass and steel. The sun in Manhattan was hardly ever bright. It always had that fuzzy yellowish hue to it because of smog, but its warmth felt good on my shoulders. I wasn't looking forward to the winter and the overarching bleakness of my apartment.

I walked to Sixth Avenue and found the Forty-Seven–Fiftieth Streets train station, a stop I rarely used. I didn't have to wait long to catch an F train down to the Lower East Side Second Avenue stop. Thanksgiving was three weeks away, yet I could sense the holiday spirit in the air. Instead of shoving me aside to get on the train, commuters shoved me and then apologized for it. The miracles had begun, and they weren't just happening on Thirty-Fourth Street.

Once off the train, I walked about eight blocks east before

turning south into a rather listless neighborhood of brick apartment buildings. Some were run-down: dingy entrances, cracked windows, the brick looking as if it hadn't been painted in about a hundred years. Others were newer, their sheen yet unaffected by the city. I found Ophelia's building—one of the older, dingier ones. The greasy lobby door was unlocked. Bits of dirt, chewing gum wrappers, and cigarette butts littered the brown-and-white tile floor along with dead leaves, neighborhood flyers, and advertising circulars. A trick had once told me to be careful on the Lower East Side, particularly on streets ruled by gangs. I wasn't sure if this was one of those streets, but I kept my eyes open just in case. He had said that if there wasn't blood in the lobby I'd probably be okay. I looked around for brownish-red spots, but didn't see any.

As I stood in front of the buzzer box, I tried hard to remember Ophelia's real name. Unless she had signed her lease under her drag name, I would be shit out of luck. I scanned the box and found a listing marked *Martin/Cox* so I decided to try it. I pushed and waited for the voice box to crackle back. Nothing. After four more tries, I figured I'd annoyed the hell out of the neighbors so I left.

I retraced my steps back to the subway, stopping for a pastrami sandwich at Katz's Delicatessen. I got back to my apartment about one p.m. and took a nap for an hour before getting ready for my shift at Han's.

Norm Han's first name was nearly unpronounceable to other Americans. Because it began with *N,* he decided to go by Norm for the benefit of his linguistically challenged friends and neighbors. I think this choice had something to do with the affable character from *Cheers,* "where everybody knows your name." But Norm didn't bear any resemblance to the television character; he was small, thin, and as energetic as a hyper lap dog. He was very happy when the holidays rolled around because he could count on a large contingent of Jewish customers visiting his establishment, as well as his nonreligious Christian and atheist regulars. Han's had won food awards from several local newspapers and had grown in popularity over the years. All of those facts had sailed over me when I applied for the job. I needed money to pay my drug-dealing landlord and I guess Norm saw something in me that he liked. Since my hiring, the restaurant had gone through a couple of waiters and food prep employees, but, for the most part, once someone got hired at Han's they were likely to stay. The family managed the restaurant well, and they were kind to their staff.

Han's could have stayed open until midnight like some Chinese eateries, but Norm called it a day around ten p.m. with the doors officially closing at eleven. By the time I got through with my shift, I was tired, but in a good way. And most of that good attitude came from Norm and the way he treated his staff and customers. People liked him and he never took advantage of his patrons or employees. If something was wrong, he made it right.

Norm came up to me about ten thirty with something in his hand. I was hoping it might be an early holiday bonus, but it was something else—a black cassette tape. I was washing some of the large platters and the heavily soiled pots by hand instead of using the sterilizer unit. My hands were in soapy water.

"A man dropped this off for you about noon," he said.

I looked at the tape and immediately got the creepy feeling something wasn't right. I studied it closely, wondering if it might explode à la *Mission Impossible*, an unlikely scenario since it had been in the building for more than ten hours.

"Who gave you this?" I asked.

"I told you. A man."

I smiled. "I know that, Norm, but could you describe him?"

He leaned against the sink and said, "He was tall—over six feet. Medium build, not an athlete, but not out of shape either."

"What about hair color, eyes?"

Norm shrugged. "He was wearing a ski cap and sunglasses."

"Did he say anything? Did he have an accent? Any distinguishing marks or characteristics?"

Norm's face screwed up into a question mark. "What are you? A private detective?"

"In a previous life," I said.

"Well, let me think about this. I was outside sweeping around the door when this guy walked up to me and said this tape was for Desde . . . Desde something."

"Desdemona."

"Yeah, that's it." Norm scratched his head. "Is that you?"

"Long story. I won't get into it now."

"Then he said, 'Cody,' so I knew who he was talking about. I didn't really pay much attention to him. He stuck the tape in my hand and walked off, toward downtown. I put it in my office and was going through receipts when I remembered I had it."

"What did he look like?"

Norm laughed and pushed away from the sink. "Better than average looking. Didn't knock my socks off, but then I don't usually go for men."

"Your loss."

"You can use my office if you want. It's unlocked. I've got a cassette player in there. I'm going back out front."

"Thanks," I said and then wiped my wet hands on my apron.

I held the tape to the side to get a better look at it in the fluorescent light. It was standard issue, the kind one could get at any record or tape store. Greasy fingerprints, probably Norm's, smeared the plastic. I walked back to the office and opened the door. Norm's inner sanctum was controlled chaos. Menus with black and red lettering were scattered across his desk, receipts were poked through a desk needle, a few spotted, white take-out bags were stuffed in the trash can. A banker's lamp threw off a sickly green light. Cookbooks and Chinese travelogues filled a case behind the desk. I guessed Norm hoped to take a trip sometime to the land of his ancestors, but never made good on the plan.

On the middle shelf, surrounded by two ruby vases etched with black dragons, was a boom box. The carry handle was broken, but it was otherwise in pretty good shape and seemed to be functional. A collection of Chinese grand opera music and 1980s rock group tapes were piled against its side. I pushed a button and one of the player lids flipped open. I inserted the tape, closed the lid, and pushed the play button.

The tape hissed through the machine, but was otherwise silent for a few seconds. I was beginning to think the whole thing was some kind of weird Rodney Jessup joke when a voice broke out through the speakers.

My skin prickled. It was not a normal voice, but one that sounded like it came from Mars or maybe Hell—Hell was more like it. It could have been male, maybe female. The voice had been altered by a modulation machine. The effect was like talking through a tin can, while waving your hand over the end farthest from the mouth.

I grabbed a paper and pen off of Norm's desk and wrote down the words that I was able to make out. I had to listen three times to get them right.

"Keep out of this. It's none of your business. Rodney Jessup is a dead man. You will be too unless you keep your nose clean." And that was it—about ten seconds of speech.

Okay.

I was pissed off. One, nobody threatened me, and two, nobody talked to me in bad detective language. *Keep your nose clean?* I don't think so.

Indeed.

It was easy to deduce that I wasn't dealing with the Mafia or any other organized gang; they didn't use tapes and voice modulation to make their point. When Jimmy Hoffa disappeared, he was gone forever, never to be seen again, no threats needed. Quick and efficient. That was the way real killers operated. This one had me worried.

Norm stuck his head in the door as I was taking the tape out of the player.

"Secret admirer?" he asked.

"Yeah. But not the kind I want."

I slid the cassette into my pocket, walked out of the office, and returned to the sink. I stuck my hands in the hot, soapy water and considered my options. I could call Rodney Jessup and ask him what was up. I could call the police and report a threat made on two lives. Or I could lie low and see what developed. The last option had the most appeal. I wasn't sure I wanted to return to all the drama that had risen like a hydra during the Combat Zone murders. I was still haunted by the memory of Chris Spinetti, former Boston police detective, blowing his brains out in the Déjà Vu, an adult film theater in Boston. I would never forget his face or the blood. And then there was Stephen, a friend I loved and later found decomposing on a mountain in New Hampshire. The pain and shock of that day sometimes came flowing back to me like taking a plunge into an icy river.

Another more frightening thought crossed my mind. This wannabe killer was an amateur, and amateurs were the worst. They had a penchant for really fucking things up, and usually taking a lot of innocent people with them. That scared the shit out of me.

Norm came back from up front with the last of the platters. I slid them into the water and washed away while plotting my next course of action. Nothing extraordinary jumped into my head. I needed a day or two to figure out what I would do. In the meantime, I'd concentrate on finding Ophelia Cox.

CHAPTER THREE

I HAD OPHELIA'S ADDRESS AND PHONE NUMBER. I called her apartment the next day about ten a.m., and the answering machine picked up again. I didn't leave a message. The thought of schlepping downtown only to stand in the lobby of Ophelia's building didn't thrill me. How could I find Ophelia in a city of seventeen million people? Plan B. I thought about where Ophelia might be if she was free for the day. Ophelia was never free, but that was another story.

Plan B called for me to visit a few local haunts—ones I suspected she might frequent. I knew these places existed, but since Stephen's death I had been a good boy. I didn't drink or do drugs anymore. I had cut back on cigarettes, weaning myself down to about three-quarters of a pack a day. Not good, but better than two packs a day. I avoided the siren call of porn theaters and strip bars and focused my energy on working out instead. I ran as much as I could—the cigarettes didn't help. And, besides, the porn theaters and strip clubs were on their way out. Rudy Giuliani was cleaning up Times Square, block by dirty block.

My midtown neighborhood was as good a place as any to find Ophelia, knowing her history of cruising for paying tricks. I could have read some Shakespeare or Marlowe, but I wasn't in the mood. I didn't think I'd run into Ophelia, but stranger things had happened. Something told me I should cruise down Eighth Avenue, walk by a couple of the bookstores, pass by the strip clubs, and maybe end up on Forty-Second Street. My gift of prophecy was kicking in big time—at least the Boston fortune-teller who'd told me I had such power might think so. If I didn't find Ophelia, maybe I'd head down to the Village for tea.

I pulled on a pair of leather pants, not exactly appropriate attire for a midmorning November stroll, but what the hell. I topped off my ensemble with a long-sleeve black T-shirt and my jean jacket, picked up my keys, and headed for the door.

I passed by the dinette table and felt the cassette tape staring at me. The sight of it sent a jolt through my body because it reminded me that a wacko knew way too much about me. The window in my kitchen didn't show much more of the outside world than people's ankles, given that my apartment was more or less underground. I lifted a slat up in the venetian blinds over the sink, and stared warily through the dirty glass and security bars. The parking spots outside were devoid of Mercedes and nobody seemed to be hanging out on the corner. My half-assed attempt at personal reconnaissance didn't give me much comfort, but I figured it was safe enough to go outside.

Forty-Seventh was filled with the usual people: grandmas toting groceries and a few teenagers hanging out on the stoop who should have been in school. I said hello to a couple of neighbors whom I had gotten to know as customers at Han's. I didn't find people in New York to be unfriendly; in fact, they were pretty nice to me. I just hadn't been in the mood to make friends.

By the time I got to Eighth, the makeup of the street had changed. The Avenue was an odd mixture of tourists wandering through the theater district, businessmen and women, along with the regular denizens of Hell's Kitchen who were barely clinging to life. I could spot them a mile away. I was in their shoes when my parents kicked me out of the house at fifteen. It didn't take long for me to turn tricks because I needed food and a place to stay.

Some of the guys looked like cheap pimps in brown suits from a bad gangster movie. Drug dealing twenty-year-olds stalked the street as well. They had that vacant zombie look on their faces, pasty white with plum-colored circles under their eyes. They were almost always dressed in dirty blue jeans and jean jackets. Then there were the hustlers, mostly young, a few good looking, but most with creased skin, greasy hair, and bad teeth. They usually hung out in the doorways or plastered themselves against a building until the proprietor told them to move on. These kids were not high-paid escorts with muscles. These were the lanky, starving boys who were kicked out of their homes because they were gay or "problem children." Some of them were orphans dropped on the street like abandoned dogs. The tragedy of these kids' lives made my stomach turn. I knew how hard it was to make a living on the street.

And how dangerous it could be.

I walked past the peep shows, the gaudy, electric, hypnotic world of sex, as enticing and addictive as opium. I half expected to see Ophelia's tall, statuesque figure gracing the door of a club. What a lady she was.

When I first met her in Boston she was like a dream, resplendent in a sleek white gown, satin gloves, and white heels. She was holding court at a drag bar in Bay Village. The club's spotlights reflected glittering sparkles on her dress and ignited a few in my eyes as well. Her skin was a mocha-chocolate brown, which made her look like a confectioner's creation, like a soda to be sipped. Her long, thin fingers with fire-engine-red nails held a mineral water laced with lime. I walked into the bar looking for a trick, and ended up leaving with a friend who taught me how to be a lady. Ophelia instructed me in the ways of superior drag: how to hide my Adam's apple, how to shave excess body hair, how to apply makeup and nails, and how to use my voice as an instrument of illusion. She became my instructor and I was her willing student. Later, I was able to mix the two aspects of my life I loved best: leather and drag. Everything I knew about becoming a woman I owed to Ophelia Cox.

Ophelia was expensive and everyone in Boston knew it. She had been turning tricks for as long as I had known her. Most drags didn't, but Ophelia learned early on in her career how to make money. She provided great service and no john ever complained. She took an occasional hit off a joint, but who didn't? Otherwise she was as clean as the US Navy pulling into port. She was rarely out of character, except when we were having sex—that was when Robert came out. Most of the time, Ophelia was "on," like a slightly demure version of Grace Jones. After a few dates, usually midweek on a slow night for johns, we'd end up in a sexual romp in one of our bedrooms. The next day, we'd spend a lazy afternoon together in each other's arms. That was how I got to know the real man behind the persona. The dresses he wore hid a slim body, thinly muscled and surprisingly fit for a drag queen. It was strange to see him out of makeup, stretched across the couch in blue jeans and a white T-shirt, his wide smile beckoning me to snuggle beside him. He was handsome with dark eyes and lashes made more dramatic by the lasting imprint of eyeliner and mascara. His face was somewhat androgynous, with strong cheekbones, but not alien or eerie in any sense. A spark flared between us, but it was extinguished by the reality of our lives. With both of us hustling, there was little time to form a lasting relationship. So, we grew apart and eventually lost touch with each other.

Then Stephen Cross came into the picture and my life changed, as our involvement and my investigation into the Combat Zone murders grew.

A few out-of-towners gathered around the entrance to a strip club to gawk and snap pictures of the gaudy interior, but Ophelia was nowhere to be seen.

I gave up on trying to find her, caught a train at Times Square, and ended up in Greenwich Village. Instead of going my normal route, I decided to explore a few side streets on my way to my favorite tea shop. I walked by the Gay and Lesbian Center where I noticed several men going inside. A banner proclaiming *Free HIV Testing* hung over the door. I'd never been in the building so I figured, what the hell, why not check it out? The door opened into an airy room with comfortable chairs and bookcases. I stood in the middle of the room and looked around. A number of hallways extended from the central lobby.

"May I help you?" a cute young man with closely cropped black hair asked.

He was sitting at a desk near the entrance. He wore a black Keith Haring T-shirt—the one with two Haring men in white outline, one humping the other.

"Just looking," I said. "I've never been inside."

"Welcome," he said in his most helpful look-no-further voice. "We offer a variety of services here: free HIV tests, other medical screenings, referrals, counseling, twelve-step groups."

My ears cocked.

"What groups, if you don't mind my asking?"

He smiled and then began in earnest, "AA, NA, SLAA, SIA, CA, MA, ACoA—"

I held up my hand. "Thanks. I get the picture."

"Here's a brochure," he said, somewhat disappointed that I had cut him off.

"How many people work here?" I asked.

"Three paid staff, I think. Most of us are volunteers."

Something prodded me to ask—it was a long shot. Even New York City didn't have that many black drags.

"Have you ever heard of someone named Ophelia Cox?"

He thought for a moment and then shook his head.

"She's a tall, thin, black drag queen, who lives on the Lower East Side. Nice looking. She usually wears white or red, her two best colors."

His eyes widened a bit. "There used to be a great drag who worked at Limelight. She looked like Diana Ross, but I haven't seen her in years. I don't know if she's the woman you're looking for."

"Thought I'd ask. If you ever hear that name could you give me a call?"

I was sure he'd ask me if I was a cop—a question straight out of a movie—but he didn't. He took down my name and number, and I left with the center's brochure tucked inside my jacket pocket.

I sauntered to my tea shop and ordered a pot of Darjeeling. As I sipped the steaming brew, I looked out on the street and wondered if I could resist Rodney Jessup's offer. On the other hand, the streets were teeming with men, a good diversion to take my mind off my troubles. I particularly salivated over a few muscle masters dressed in leather. A charge shot through my groin. It had been more than a year since I'd had really good sex with a man. For the first time in a long time I was getting horny. That was dangerous.

A couple of days passed without any contact from Rodney Jessup, the creep who handed Norm the tape, or the cute boy from the center. In the meantime, my head seemed to be centered on my crotch, but rubbing one off didn't seem to cut it. I jokingly told Norm about my predicament one night at work.

He took my soapy hands in his and said with mock seriousness, "I feel your pain, but don't look to me to solve your problem." I laughed at his joke.

The next morning, I got a phone call. I answered with some trepidation because I instinctively felt it might be bad news. It wasn't. My prophecy genes hadn't been performing so well lately.

"Cody?" the voice asked.

I didn't immediately recognize the caller.

"This is Brian . . . from the center. I've been trying to reach you."

I perked up. "Brian. Thanks for calling. I work nights, and I don't have a machine."

"Oh?" he asked.

Apparently, my lack of technology had dropped me a few notches in his estimation.

"I've got news for you. I asked a couple of friends who live on the East Side if they've ever heard of Ophelia Cox. One of them has." He stopped, waiting for me to respond.

"That's great, Brian. Where can I find her?"

"Well, my friend's never seen Ophelia in drag, but he knew the name immediately."

"That'll do. At least it's a lead."

Brian sighed. "Look, you're not going to do anything bad, like arrest her, right? I mean, you're not a cop, are you?"

I couldn't help but laugh, but the questions were serious, and I admired him for standing up for Ophelia. "Don't worry, Brian, she and I are old friends—former lovers, to be exact. I think she may need help. That's why I'm looking for her. Besides, I gave you my name and number. If I was out to get her, I wouldn't be that stupid."

"Guess so," Brian said. "She hangs out at Club Leo on Delancey Street. I think she works as a bar back."

I was surprised Ophelia might be hauling dirty glasses and dishes at a club, but then I wasn't one to talk. I thanked Brian and hung up. My next evening off was Thursday night. I'd have to wait until then to check out Club Leo.

I asked a neighborhood gay couple who came into Han's for a bite, if they knew anything about Club Leo. One had lived in the Lower East Side for a couple of years before moving to Hell's Kitchen. He said the bar began its life as Club Leo, a hangout for locals, then changed ownership and became a gay club for a year. It didn't last long because no uptown queens wanted to venture to Delancey Street, so the club converted back to Club Leo and became mixed. About a year ago, punks had taken it over and since then it operated successfully as a venue for area punk revival bands.

I left my apartment about eleven o'clock on Thursday night and caught the train downtown. Because I had been forewarned, I dressed head to toe in leather. I avoided makeup, but put on a pair of white-laced combat boots for effect.

When I arrived, a small crowd of young men and women—most dressed in black, accented with silver chains and loops—stood smoking and talking outside the door in the cold, spitting rain.

Club Leo was a standard Lower East Side joint. The building was painted black. There were no windows on its front, only an equally dark door framed on both sides by two painted orange lions that faced each other like ornamental bookends. As I got closer, I could hear the music blaring inside, as the door pulsed with the frenetic beat. I steeled myself for the noise, pushed past the crowd, and stepped inside.

A garish purple light flooded the club. A band of three men and one woman hammered out a frantic song about carpentry tools and death on a tiny stage at the back of the building.

The lyrics went something like, "Nails . . . die! Screwdriver . . . die! Hammer . . . die!" Probably the opening act for the evening.

A few band groupies were dancing like lunatics in front of the stage. I worked my way toward the bar on the left hand side of the room, afraid if I got closer to the stage my eardrums would burst into uncontrolled bleeding.

A red-haired, tough bartender, attired in skintight button-fly jeans eyed me as I approached. His ample pectorals glistened in the weird light. A pair of wide suspenders stretched over his flat stomach, bare chest, and shoulders. A couple of the buttons at his crotch were strategically popped open, which I found titillating, particularly when he bent over. He was a butch guy who didn't smile much, but he clearly didn't mind giving a show to the paying customers.

"Water," I shouted.

He frowned. Not much of a tip on a bottle of water.

He reached under the counter, pulled out a chilled one, and put it on top of a white bar napkin. I paid him, generously tipping for the erotic thoughts, and retreated to a back corner. As I stood there listening to the band rave on, I considered how crazy it was to be in a punk bar at midnight on a Thursday. My life was sedate these days. Sedate in the truest sense of the word. I would rather have been at home reading some new plays by Sam Shepard. I sighed and sipped my water.

As I stood there watching the band play, a tall black man at the right side of the stage caught my eye. He was carrying a plastic bucket filled with ice, and was headed toward the exhibitionist bartender. I couldn't be certain that it was Ophelia—this man looked much thinner than I remembered—but I had to find out.

I walked to the bar and stood next to him. He was wearing jeans, a black T-shirt, and fluorescent orange earplugs.

He handed the bucket to the bartender, who dumped the ice into a cooler under the counter.

The man looked at me with no hint of recognition.

I put my hand on his shoulder and he jumped. A lick of fear shot through his eyes, then they narrowed and focused on my face. The skin on his forehead crept up slightly, but he said nothing. He turned and skulked away.

"Ophelia!" I started after him, but was held back by the bartender's hand that grabbed the back of my jacket.

"Shit," I said to him. "Let go. I've been trying to find my friend, Robert, for days."

"Look, buddy," the bartender said while tightening his grip. "The employees got work to do. We don't talk to the customers other than to take orders. If you want to see him, you can do it when he's off the clock."

I had two twenty-dollar bills and the change from the ten I had broken for the water in my pocket. I pulled out the two twenties and waved them in front of his face.

He thought about my bribe for about a second before he grabbed the money and stuffed it in his jean pocket. "Five minutes," he said. "That's all. More than that and I'll throw you out."

Like hell. I decided to let it go and not waste time.

I rushed after the man who had disappeared in back of a curtain to the right of the stage. I ducked behind it as well and found myself in a narrow hall that led past a couple of dingy dressing rooms to a small area that I assumed served as a green room and employee lounge.

I found him, his head cupped in his hands, sitting on a dilapidated folding chair. The earplugs lay on the table like orange bugs. The band's noise was less audible here; an ice machine thrummed in the corner. At least it was quiet enough we could talk.

I touched his back and he shivered under his T-shirt. He lowered his hands, turned to me, and looked at me with tear-streaked eyes.

"Des," he said softly, "I wanted it to be you, but . . . "

"Talk to me, Ophelia," I said.

"I'm sick, Des. Deathly sick."

"I know."

I leaned toward him. He pressed his head against my shoulder and cried.

I wrested an extra five minutes from the bartender. Robert told me that he did live in the building I had visited in the Lower East Side, not far from the club. We promised to meet late the next morning at my favorite tea shop in Greenwich Village. The shop was a halfway meeting point for us.

When Robert walked in the door, he looked composed, more like the man I had known several years ago in Boston. We sat at a table in the front window and watched pedestrians pass by. The sun broke free from the clouds now and then and splashed the table with light. The warm rays felt good on my body.

"Tell me everything," I said.

"How did you find me?" he asked.

"Win Hart told me you were in New York. I hope that's okay. You know Win could never keep a secret. But I also asked a guy at the Gay and Lesbian Center, and he was the one who led me to you."

He smiled and his simple expression brought back memories of Boston and pleasant afternoons together when life was easier.

"Yes, Win once told me you killed a man," Robert said.

"Shit, you know that's not true."

Those distinctive dark eyebrows rose.

"He was a trick," I said, "and he was murdered by the Combat Zone Killer."

The waiter brought our tea, and Robert poured a cup for himself. His hand shook a bit as he held the pot.

"I read about it later," he said. "The whole business was nasty." He brought the cup to his lips and looked absentmindedly out the window. "I'm sorry about Stephen," he said in almost a whisper. "I know how much you cared for him."

"True," I said, "but life goes on and time heals—"

"Spare me the platitudes, Des. You don't have to suck it up for me." He turned from the window and his lips narrowed in an angry frown. "I don't want to hear about healing or how life goes on because I don't have much time on this lovely little spinning ball. You're well read—much more than I. You've studied the classics. You know tragedy when you see it."

This was a side of Robert I'd never seen, and I didn't know how to react. The Robert Martin I remembered was smooth and sexy, not angry and bitter. As Ophelia, she was comfortable holding a martini in one hand and a bejeweled cigarette holder in the other. Ophelia was classy even when she was working the Déjà Vu.

"I'm sorry," I said. "I didn't mean to be flip." I looked at him squarely. "So how did this happen, and, more importantly, how can I help?"

He took a sip of tea and then put his cup on the saucer. "It's a long, boring story full of rage and tears."

"I've got time."

"Well, how long has it been since we've seen each other?"

"About two years, I guess."

He reached across the table and patted my hand. "Too long. I'll make it the *Reader's Digest* condensed version." He leaned back in his chair. "The city was closing down the Zone before the murders started. I know it sounds weird, but I felt comfortable there."

"Not at all," I said. "I know—the Combat Zone felt like home to me, too."

"I was making money, and I knew my limits. When I was in public, oddly enough, my vices were more controlled. When things went south in the Zone after the killings, the business shifted. I started getting calls for Boston hotels and Back Bay parties. At first, I was thrilled. The money was great and the men were—what should I say—a higher class. At least, that's what I thought.

"But something else was creeping into my life. These high

rollers could afford a lot more than just me. A lot of white powder appeared out of nowhere, usually spread across a table—and then came the needles."

Robert rolled up the sleeve of his shirt and showed me his right arm.

I winced.

His chocolate skin was pockmarked with purplish scars.

"The left arm is worse," he said. "I got hooked. I was high all the time and I made some bad choices. I've been clean for a while now, but the damage was done. Now, I've got *the* disease—the unholy badge of honor that's sapping all my strength and all my resources. I didn't get it from sex. I got it from sharing needles." He stopped and stared out the window again. "I wonder which sin is greater?"

"I'm sorry." What else could I say?

We could have carried on about choices and responsibilities and how sorry we were that life turned out the way it did, but none of that seemed to matter in that moment. Robert was a friend who needed what little help I could provide.

He tapped his fingernails on the table. "You know what? I feel like splurging." He pointed to the baked goods that were pleasingly arranged behind a long glass display case. "I'm going to order one of those delicious chocolate-chip muffins. I've had my eye on it ever since we came in."

"Get what you want," I said. "I'm buying."

"Oh, no you're not. I'm not broke yet—soon to be, but not yet. It's sad when life comes down to a muffin or the cost of a pill."

I couldn't let a friend down. "I'm not rich either, but I can pay for tea and a muffin."

I called the waiter over and ordered the muffin.

Robert's lips opened in a broad smile and he asked, "Do you believe in God?"

I shook my head.

"I'm in a twelve-step program," he said. "That was one of the reasons I moved to New York from Boston. More anger about AIDS, better services for those who can't afford it. I'm still sorting all this spiritual stuff out—God and all that. There's something to be said for it. I've seen some miraculous recoveries. I'm hoping . . . "

I wanted to believe he was right. "Maybe it'll work for you."

The waiter placed a gigantic muffin in front of Robert. The chocolate had melted into a delicious goo in the microwave.

"I haven't gotten over the anger yet," he said. "Sometimes I feel like there's no God at all. 'Hey, is anybody there?' It's like *He* shuffled off to Buffalo a long time ago and left us alone to fend for ourselves. God is like an absent landlord—never around but still expects the rent to be paid."

I caught sight of a black Mercedes cruising by the window. It wasn't Rodney Jessup's, but it reminded me that there was a whole lot of money waiting for me if I wanted to accept his offer. Tainted money, one might call it, because of the bounty on Stephen Cross's head.

"Maybe I can work something out for you," I said. "How badly do you need cash?"

Robert laughed. "This girl is black and poor. I need money for rent, food, and drugs. Real, life-saving drugs."

"Give me a little time."

He took a huge bite of the muffin and between swallows, said, "Des, I can always count on you."

I smiled. "We have a history, Ophelia. I'm not going to let it end over a muffin."

A mist crept into his eyes, and he nodded. My next step would be to call Rodney Jessup and tell him I was interested in his proposition. A hell of a lot of cash was at stake. And beyond that, it didn't hurt that Rodney's hunky bodyguard popped into my mind every now and then, usually undressed. The siren call of caution beckoned to me, but my head told it to take a flying leap. Rodney's money might be the cure for Ophelia, but it also might be the death of me.

FOUR

NORM SCOWLED WHEN I TOLD HIM I MIGHT NEED A few days off.

"You've got to be kidding, Cody." He put a tub full of dirty dishes next to the sink.

"Seriously, Norm. You know I wouldn't ask for the time if I didn't need it. How many days have I taken off in a year and a half?"

Norm scrunched up his lips and moved them side to side in thought. "I guess about three."

"See? By your own admission, I've been getting screwed when it comes to vacation time."

Norm laughed. "You know we don't have vacation time here. You just don't get paid."

"It's about the tape. I've got some business to attend to before it turns nasty."

His eyes brightened and I could see the excitement from my predicament take over his imagination. "Okay," he said, "but let me know ASAP. I'll have to get my sister-in-law in here to wash dishes and it won't be pretty."

I had met the woman a few times and he was right. Menial labor did not become her.

The next morning, I picked up the phone with the intention of calling Rodney Jessup. I punched in about three numbers from his business card and then my fingers froze.

I had tried so hard since Stephen's death to isolate myself, and, for the most part, I had succeeded and enjoyed the slow ride down life's highway. I said no to drama—other than reading my favorite playwrights—and I hadn't regretted it. There was something to be said for safety and security.

But by dialing his number, by jumping into the fire, I would once again turn my world upside down. The months of lazing in my apartment would be history. The routine of a job, a good night's sleep, and a run in Central Park, had become seductive, as addictive as any controlled substance I had ever imbibed. What had become of my man of action? I was suffering from what every American seems to want: a nice quiet life without too much stress.

When Stephen Cross was kidnapped, I had a good reason to search for him. In my way, I loved the man and he was a good, good friend. Stephen and I never had sex—not that I didn't want to—but he was in a monogamous relationship when we met. Ophelia was different, but she was a friend, too. With both these men, layers of friendship twisted and turned in bizarre ways that kept us connected throughout our histories. Ophelia was more than a teacher of drag to me. She was a person I respected and wanted to help. When John Dresser asked me to look for Stephen, the decision had been easy. I struggled with this one, but when I thought about it, I had no choice but to dial Jessup's number. Having some cash on hand wouldn't be bad either.

Rodney's voice sounded jittery when he answered the phone, like he'd been on an all-night bender.

"Stress getting to you, Reverend?" I asked.

Rodney paused as if stung by my comment and finally said, "Do you have a soul, Mr. Harper? Because if you do, you would understand the pain that's being inflicted on my family. Can you really be that heartless?"

I wasn't in the mood for tea and sympathy. "If the job is still open, I want it." He exhaled and I continued. "I can't guarantee that I'm the answer to your problems—"

"When can you be here?"

"Tomorrow."

"Good. Book a flight to Richmond. I'll have a driver pick you up."

"Am I staying overnight?"

"Pack a bag."

"There's just one little thing. I want half up front, the other half when I complete the job—whenever that is. Finding someone, as you put it."

I expected some hesitation, but there was none. He asked for the account number at my bank. I had no problem giving it to him because there was less than five hundred dollars in it. That was a fortune to me, a pittance to him.

Two hundred and fifty thousand dollars would be there by the end of the business day, he said. I told him I would book the flight once the cash was in.

"Don't bother, I've changed my mind. I'll make the reservation for you. I'm sending a car tomorrow morning to take you to LaGuardia. If there's a problem call me."

We hung up and I flopped on my couch, flabbergasted. I suddenly had more money coming to me than I had ever dreamed of. Rodney Jessup was about to make me a rich man.

The day dragged by. I called Ophelia and told her I had landed a big job and not to worry about getting money for meds. If everything went according to plan, there would be enough money for spa treatments in addition to medical treatments, and then some left over for several nice cruises.

I called Norm and told him that I wasn't coming in to work and would be out for at least a week. He groused a bit, but said my job would be waiting for me when I came back. Suddenly, I was able to fulfill everyone's fantasy of thumbing my nose at the boss and walking out the door. But I couldn't do that to Norm. I'd return to Han's if only to work out my notice.

I rummaged in my closet trying to find something decent to wear to Virginia. I guessed the Commonwealth might be warmer than New York City, but I really had no idea where I was going. I pulled out all my leather and laughed. Chaps and a leather jock-strap might be fun, but probably weren't appropriate attire for Rodney, or whatever else might come up in Virginia. Drag didn't seem like a good choice either. Nothing I owned really made sense.

Finally, I dug out a decent piece of luggage I'd found on the street near Columbus Circle and started to pack—a shaving kit, underwear, for decency's sake, and toiletries. For a moment, I had to stop, pinch myself, and ask if this was really happening. The money didn't come without risk, but a quarter of a million dollars?

A bank account was one of the little luxuries I'd never had before coming to New York. I had to produce ID and go through all the standard procedure of opening an account. The nice people there even gave me a secured credit card with a five hundred dollar limit—since I had no credit history. My meager savings backed it up.

I looked through my closet, and decided that a trip to Macy's was in order. After a nice lunch, I purchased some chinos, a few shirts, a handsome jacket, a pair of sunglasses, as well as a pair of gloves and a scarf. Three hours later, my card was four hundred dollars poorer, but I was richer in street clothes. I was beginning to feel like a real person, and I liked it.

On the way home, I strode into my bank with my red and white bags in hand. The assistant manager who opened my account usually gave me a nod and a quick hello, but this time he broke into a wide grin, rose from his desk, practically skipped toward me, and shook my hand.

"So nice to see you again, Mr. Harper," he said.

He was a portly Hispanic man whose face flushed at the sight of me. "I just wanted you to know that your wire came in safely. If there's anything we can do to keep your business, let us know. Thank you for trusting us with your deposit."

"That's why I came in," I said. "I wanted to know if all two hundred and—"

He put a finger to his lips. "I would say you're a *quarter* richer than you were this morning."

"That's good to know," I said. "Take care of it."

He laughed and his stomach jiggled underneath his white shirt.

I walked out of the bank into the sunshine. I put on my new sunglasses and looked up at the towers around me. A song broke out inside my head: "Money," from *Cabaret*. The world was indeed going round at a dizzying pace.

My view of life was changing dramatically. And it was all happening so fast.

My alarm went off at five a.m.

Forty-five minutes later, my apartment buzzer blared with an annoying metallic ring. I peered through the blinds and looked to the right, toward the set of stairs that led down to my door. The light over the door threw its feeble rays on a figure in crisp black pants and polished shoes who stood waiting for an answer.

I looked to the street. A long, black limo was double-parked in front of my building.

I went to the door. "Who is it?"

"Your driver," a rather stiff voice replied.

"I didn't ask for a driver," I said to throw him off. I wanted to make sure he was legitimate.

"I know, sir. Mr. Jessup ordered a car service . . . to ensure that you make it to the airport on time."

"That's very thoughtful of Reverend Jessup. I was going to take the shuttle bus. Are you armed?"

"No, sir!" came the shocked reply.

I unlocked the door, but kept the security chain on. My driver, a middle-aged man with salt-and-pepper hair, looked harmless enough. "Give me a minute."

I shut the door in his face, and walked through the apartment one more time. I had never been on a jet in my life and, suddenly, I was getting nervous. The thought of flying at thirty-two thousand feet with nothing under me but air turned my stomach upside down. What the hell was happening? Was I a neurotic mess because I had something to lose? Maybe it was my sudden bankroll of close friends who happened to be residing in my account. I used to be fearless. The whole terrible tragedy with Stephen Cross, Chris Spinetti, Carl Roy, and Rodney Jessup ran through my mind. My life had become much too comfortable, and I was no longer used to stepping out of my comfort zone. I thought about what Helen Keller once said about security being an illusion for every creature on earth. I might as well live dangerously. I grabbed my bag and opened the door.

"This way," the driver said.

I carried my bag to the stoop, locked the door, and looked lovingly at the apartment buildings down the street. I missed them already.

"Allow me, sir," the man said and picked up the bag.

He walked to the car with my luggage and opened the rear door. I ducked inside and settled onto a black leather seat. The interior was warm, and gentle string music played over the stereo speakers. The trunk release popped and then closed. The driver got into the front and pulled away from the curb.

A short time later, his voice came through the speakers over the music. "Help yourself to orange juice and bagels if you like. Just push the button in front of you."

I jabbed the button as instructed and a burled walnut panel slid open. A chilled bottle of orange juice sat inside the compartment along with cinnamon raisin bagels and cream cheese. Rodney was putting on the dog for me. I picked up a chilled glass, poured some juice, and leaned back in the comfortable seat. Soon, we were gliding east through the Midtown Tunnel on our way to Queens.

We arrived at the airport about an hour and half before my flight took off. The driver escorted me to the luxurious flight lounge, which seemed like a classy hotel lobby. It was comfortable, quiet, and well-appointed, with leather chairs and several televisions. Passengers could select from coffee, tea, pastries, water, or snacks for their breakfast pleasure. I watched the morning news, along with men in blue business suits and starched white shirts and women in equally dapper jackets, skirts, and heels. Soon, an agent handed me a ticket and informed me I'd be boarding as a first-class passenger, which was a pleasant surprise. Fortunately, I was dressed in my new chinos and a button-down shirt rather than my usual T-shirt and jeans.

After boarding, I strapped myself into my seat and tried to focus on enjoying the flight. My first time flying was turning out to be quite the adventure, after all. That line of thinking kept me calm until the plane took off. My heart raced along with the jet engines. I looked out my passenger window to see the streets of Queens and Manhattan sink below me. In seconds, we were over the East River. Looking south, I saw the Empire State Building and the World Trade Center rise like monoliths, their tops skirting the early morning clouds. In a short time, we were over the industrial wastelands of Jersey and headed south to the Piedmont region of

Richmond. I sank into my seat, closed my eyes, and tried to nap.

A driver carrying a sign marked *Harper* met me at the Richmond airport. He led me to my second limo ride in a day. This car was stocked with a full bar of nips. I couldn't decide whether Jessup was trying to get me drunk or just tempt me. Either way, the man of God certainly knew how to put the itch under my skin. I lit a cigarette, hit the button on the arm console, and cracked the window. We drove west for about an hour and a half across rolling hills before traversing a mountain range. We skirted a small town called Buena Vista. In each direction there were green peaks awash in pale blue. The driver told me Rodney Jessup's home was about three miles from the center of town.

The limo wound its way through densely wooded areas of pine and tall oaks, thrusting us into alternating patterns of shadow and sun. I knew we were nearing Rodney's home when the car slowed and turned right down a road bordered on each side by cedars, maples, and stands of tall pines. Soon, we came to a stop in front of an ornate wrought-iron gate. The initials RJ were fashioned into the top. Two gilt stone lions sat looking at us from atop their perches of red brick. The gate split open and we slipped through. We drove at least a half mile down the road before the house came into view.

To describe the house as large would be an understatement. The red brick colonial, with immense side wings, stretched the length of the mountain base it sat upon. The land around the structure was cleared, but the tree line was so close it gave the inhabitants privacy in every direction. A large white-columned portico, which would be particularly useful in winter snows, graced the circular drive. The car glided to a stop under it and the driver came around and opened the door. He then took my bag from the trunk as the front door to the house opened with a slow creak.

The person who greeted me was not Rodney Jessup. She was a

young Hispanic woman with dark hair and even darker eyes, and I assumed she was part of Jessup's household staff. She welcomed me as I entered the house, and she led me to a living room that was straight out of *House Beautiful*, not to mention the killer view of the lush landscaped grounds that stretched to the base of the mountain.

The most striking feature of the room was the gigantic stone fireplace that took up nearly half a wall. Floor-to-ceiling glass framed it. That architectural element gave the effect of being outside at a campfire, when in actuality you were seated comfy and cozy in one of the zillion chairs and sofas scattered about the room. I noticed the fabric label on one of them. Scalamandré, of course.

"Reverend Jessup will be in to see you in a moment," the woman said. "Lunch will be served soon."

"Thank you . . . uh . . . "

"Abby," she replied.

She turned and left me alone with my bag, which the driver had deposited near my chair.

"Thank you, Abby," I said to the empty room.

Jessup didn't keep me waiting long enough to feel like a second-class citizen, but my arms were getting itchy by the time he appeared. To pass the time, I looked at Christian magazines, many featuring interviews with Rodney, enough to fill my lifetime quota.

Finally, he sauntered in from the left wing. He looked considerably more relaxed than the last time I saw him, when he was parked outside my apartment in New York.

He wore blue slacks and an expensive maroon cashmere sweater over a white shirt. His hair looked a touch darker than I remembered from our meeting at the church in Manchester, New Hampshire. Perhaps in preparation for announcing his bid for president he had indulged in a dye job. Cosmetic aids certainly weren't out of his range of vanity. His face was a soft pink. In the light that filtered in through the large windows he looked to be in good health.

At first, I didn't notice someone was walking behind him. But when Rodney took a few steps down to the living room, a swarthy face popped into view. He was the driver I'd seen in New York, Rodney's bodyguard. He carried himself confidently with a touch of swagger and was dressed in a double-breasted black suit complemented by a muted checked tie. His muscular body was almost bursting under the fabric. Clearly, this man was no stranger to the gym or he had unbelievable genes. I couldn't help but notice the outline of a shoulder holster underneath his suit. That wasn't the only outline that attracted my attention; his pants were bunched at the crotch. He was packing heat there as well. His velvety brown eyes took me in as I sat transfixed in the chair.

"Mr. Harper." Rodney extended his hand. Because I was his reluctant employee I chose to shake it. "I trust your trip went well."

"Yes," I said. "I didn't expect the royal treatment, but as long as you're buying I'm happy."

"You're under my employ as of now," he said and looked down at me with a smile that smacked of condescension.

I was about to reply when he turned and introduced the stud who was waiting patiently behind him like a trained bear.

"This is Anthony Vargas," Rodney said. "He used to work for the local police department, but he's a private investigator now."

"Oh, a private dick," I said and rose to shake Mr. Vargas's hand. "I've been wondering who you were—actually more than wondering." I couldn't help but snicker.

"Pleased to meet you, Cody," he said and then smiled.

I melted a little when he clasped my hand. Horns sprouted out of my head.

"We can talk over lunch," Rodney said and pointed to the dining room situated to the right down the hall.

Abby had apparently sneaked in with the salads when I wasn't looking. Rodney sat at the head of a large mahogany table. Anthony and I took places across from each other. I chose the seat with the view of the expansive lawn. Soon, Abby appeared with a carafe of white wine. She served Rodney a generous glass.

The dick and I said a polite, "No, thanks."

"So, Reverend Jessup, let's get to the point," I said. "I get the feeling you need to fill me in on a whole lot of history before we get to the purpose of my job."

Rodney sipped his wine and then placed his fork on the salad plate. "Tony has been on the job a bit longer than you, so I'll let him explain."

So, it was Tony. Not only did Rodney hire a looker, he was on a nickname basis with him as well.

"Okay, Tony," I said. "Spill."

Tony was not outwardly amused at my pseudo command. However, I detected a ripple of laughter behind the irises. I wasn't sure, but I thought he liked me. I was jumping the gun a bit. I wasn't even certain he was a friend of Dorothy's, but my gaydar was getting positive returns from the hunk across the table.

Tony had only poked at his salad. He sipped his water and began. "You might remember that two men were shot in the head near the National Zoo last April."

I nodded. I had seen the newspaper story in a coffee shop near my apartment and made a mental note of the murders at the time. Oddly enough, that mention occurred the day the paper ran a big front-page headline about the burgeoning Jessup sex scandal.

"Both of those men worked behind the scenes for Reverend Jessup's campaign," Tony said. "The murders were never solved, but the threats against his campaign and his family continued during the subsequent chain of events . . . ." Tony looked at

Rodney as if he needed permission to continue.

"It's all right," Rodney said. "It was a scandal. It knocked me out of the race and ruined everything I hold dear in life—except my bank account."

"You've become strangely materialistic, Reverend, since we last met," I said. "In Manchester, you were much holier-than-thou."

"Money is all I have left," Rodney said. "Nothing was ever proven when I was crucified in the press, yet the innuendo and the murder of Stephen Cross were enough to ruin my political career."

Rodney had no compunction about dredging up crap that made me boil. "You conveniently seem to forget the business card you dropped at the Hercules Theater."

I had to hand it to Jessup. Maybe it was the wine, or he knew the position I was in—ass in the air—but he remained calm.

"A business card found by a reporter with my thumb print on it. How novel. I've done thousands of interviews. How am I supposed to remember a meeting with a small-time newspaperman in New Haven years before my campaign began? Life is full of lost memories and coincidences. And setups."

"Are you suggesting that Stephen set *you* up?" I was ready to go for his throat.

"Please," Tony said, becoming the voice of reason. "We're not accomplishing anything. Let's get back to the facts."

Rodney and I stared at each other warily, while Tony waited until I cooled off.

"Things were fine for a while after Reverend Jessup withdrew from the campaign," Tony said. "But within the past couple of months the threats have escalated—vandalism outside the property, late-night phone calls—untraceable, of course. Some pretty disturbing stuff."

"What kind of vandalism?" I asked.

Rodney sighed and took a gulp of wine.

"Blood on the entrance gate," Tony said. "A fetus left in a bag on the driveway."

"Human?" I asked.

"Certainly not," Rodney said. "We're not dealing with murder on this property, and I want no part of that."

"Both were from a pig," Tony said.

I munched a bit of salad. The fresh greens and vegetables were good, but I didn't feel hungry. This lunch was too much like consorting with the enemy.

"Security cameras?" I asked Tony.

"Around the perimeter of the property, but the perp knew enough about cameras to know their range and color capabilities. All the cameras caught was a dark, unidentifiable blur."

"Any clues from the bag or fetus?"

"Store bought," Tony said. "Nothing that couldn't be found in any hardware or butcher shop."

Rodney pointed his fork at me. "But there have also been letters threatening my life, mailed from New York City."

"Don't flatter yourself, Reverend," I said. "If I'd wanted revenge it would have happened a long time ago."

"I never suspected you," Rodney said. "You're oddly moral for a *homosexual*. A strong sense of duty and friendship can be an asset, or a liability, depending on the man. I don't believe you are a killer."

"Only when pushed," I said. "I also have a strong sense of self-preservation."

"Carol and the children have left the house," Rodney said. "Both Tony and I felt they would be safer if they were elsewhere. Of course, it creates a huge hardship for our family."

Abby appeared to my right and took away the half-eaten salads. She asked me if I would like chicken or fish for the entrée. I was in the mood for fish.

"I guess that brings us to suspects," I said. "Who wants to kill you, Reverend? And why?"

I thought Rodney was going to choke on his wine. He snorted and then came up for air. "Let's see." His blue eyes darkened in a contained fury. "Everyone in the Council for Religious Advancement, about every member of the Beacon of God Churches, all the big donors to my presidential campaign, every homosexual in Boston . . . shall I go on?"

"You've made your point," I said. I cast a glance at Tony who seemed as disgusted by his employer's display as I was. "I'm talking about real suspects—not everyone who thinks you're an asshole."

Rodney's eyes flashed. "Some people still respect me. Fortunately, my wife and children are among those."

"So Tony," I said. "What have you come up with?"

Tony shifted in his seat. "I've worked probably a hundred leads, but nothing's panned out. Someone has it in for Reverend Jessup, and I believe he or she is dangerous."

"Interesting," I said. "Could be a woman. Women have been known to carry a grudge."

Abby appeared with lunch. My appetite had picked up somewhat, so I ate what I could stomach. It was a hell of a lot easier looking at Tony than the white fish laid out on my plate. By the time dessert came, I had him undressed in my head. If Tony was strapped to my bed, naked, would he look anything like my fantasy? We dropped the detective talk for a bit, while Rodney rhapsodized about his love affair with Virginia, his church, and his family, in that order.

When we got back to business, I asked, "How is your relationship with Carol?"

"My wife and I are on the best of terms," he said, "and I'd prefer if you'd keep her out of this."

"Nothing's off limits, Reverend," I countered. "Which brings up a question. Why did you hire me? You hinted at the reason the night you camped out in front of my apartment, but I wasn't up for company."

"Because you're not a member of law enforcement. I hired you for the same reason I presume Stephen Cross did. You're smart and you know the street. You may be able to sniff something out that our friend Tony might not."

"Stephen didn't hire me," I said. "I worked for Stephen because . . . we were good friends. But you're right, I can sometimes see things cops can't. I have a certain way of looking at things." I gazed at Tony. "In fact, I never liked cops."

Tony smiled and said, "I'm the one who found you for Reverend Jessup."

I smiled back and Tony's eyes twinkled. "Congratulations on your initiative. I think we're going to enjoy working together."

"It was easy, really," Tony said.

He unbuttoned his suit jacket and leaned back in his chair. His pecs strained against his white shirt. His nipples made perfect round circles underneath the fabric. His service revolver reared its shiny black butt from under his left armpit.

I smiled back. "Easy. I like that word. Here in the South, living should be *easy*."

Tony nodded.

I wondered how easy he was.

CHAPTER
FIVE

RODNEY, TONY, AND I SPENT THE DAY DISCUSSING
leads. Frankly, nothing struck me, except the disturbing fact that
Rodney, for a man of God, had made a lot of enemies. They were
of all kinds, too—political, social, and religious. I couldn't discount
dissension within his ranks. I remembered the plump woman in
New Hampshire who wanted so desperately to get a glimpse of
Jessup when he made his presidential announcement. She had told
me about an unidentified woman who had thrown herself years ago
at Jessup in a New Orleans hotel room. The good reverend had the
woman removed from the conference. I'm sure she was banished
from his sight forever, hiding her head in shame like some biblical
harlot, cleansed of her demons by Rodney, like countless others.

After dinner, I was getting antsy and even a bit claustrophobic
in the big house. Tony stifled a few yawns and made leaving
noises. I had been up early for the flight and the day was beginning to catch up with me.

Rodney talked away about old times and slouched in his leather
wing chair, a victim of too many scotch and sodas at dinner.

He offered to take us to breakfast at a Buena Vista restaurant so Abby could have a respite from the kitchen. That, of course, presumed that he'd be sober enough to drive by then.

Tony shook my hand and said good night. He said he would meet us at the restaurant. I was sorry to see him leave. I'd hoped that he was staying with Jessup also and that we had adjoining suites or at least rooms across the hall from each other. But my fantasy was shot to hell. I assumed Abby was in the house some-where or had slipped home after the last of Rodney's cocktails.

My bag had disappeared sometime after lunch, but I wasn't too worried. It showed up in the room Jessup led me to in the right wing of the house, nearest the kitchen and dining room. My guest bedroom was plush by any standard. The fabrics were soft and luxurious. The curtained windows looked out on the back lawn, which was illuminated by security lights. The grass still looked healthy and green even for November. A large four-poster bed called to me. There was a gigantic TV on a walnut dresser. The bathroom contained a whirlpool tub and the usual standard items. Everything was perfect. Too perfect.

Rodney said he'd wake me up at seven a.m. He closed the door and I locked it. I pulled the drapes, stripped, and stepped into the whirlpool tub. I soaked for about thirty minutes in the hot, bubbling water until I was limp all over. I dried myself with one of the plush towels and looked in the mirror. A small ridge was forming around my waist and I didn't like it. The fat probably was coming from all the free dinners I got at Han's. I pinched the fleshy band hoping it was under an inch. Barely. My face looked flushed from the bath and I was happy to be rid of the ponytail, which I'd cut about six months before. The crew cut suited me. I was going through this self-indulgent exercise for Tony's sake. I wanted to make sure I was presentable—naked. I was about as good as I could get at my age, just under thirty-five.

I crawled into bed and slept soundly. Usually, I slept with one eye open, but tonight, the trip, the drive, and the exhausting day with Rodney overtook me.

The hand pulling down the blanket woke me up. I jolted awake, turned, and grabbed at the wrist over my back. I hadn't heard a thing when the door opened.

It was Rodney.

I pushed him away. "What the hell are you doing?"

"I just wanted to talk," he said.

The *l* in talk disappeared in a boozy slur. The acrid stench of consumed scotch wafted from his breath.

I lifted myself up in bed. The covers fell away revealing my chest and stomach. I never wore pajamas. "We can talk at breakfast." I could have easily pounced and thrown him from the room. Mostly, I felt sorry for him, having had my own run-ins with addiction.

He tried to walk toward me but stumbled, landing in a fit of laughter at the foot of my bed. He was wearing a thin white robe, which revealed more than I wanted to see from my employer. He curled his legs up and covered himself.

"Okay, Rodney, what's up? Why the nocturnal visit?" I looked at the clock on the nightstand. It was after two.

"I wanted to say hi." He waved at me.

He was truly smashed. I had dealt with similar situations before. The best tactic was to let the drunk have his say until he passed out or let him talk himself out until I could escort him back to his room. That was the best course of action. Another option would have been to take advantage of him. Many a drunken visit from "straight" men—*Christ, was I drunk last night* syndrome—came about from excessive alcohol consumption. However, the fact that many women and quite a few men had thrown themselves at Rodney did not make him attractive to me. He was still reprehensible in my book. I was somewhat flattered, though, to get the chance, from a celebrity fuck perspective.

"You didn't really come to say hi," I said. "What do you want?"

He smiled and his head bobbed like those toys some idiots paste on the dashboards of their cars.

"Do you think I'm attractive?"

What to answer? No, and he'd be a blubbering mess. Yes, and he'd be all over me.

"Personally, I think you're attractive to many people, but I think we're just friends." I lied about the friends part, but Rodney wouldn't remember the conversation anyway.

"Stephen Cross found me attractive."

I leaned back against the pillow, stunned at his admission.

"Are you telling me that you and Stephen had sex?"

He nodded in his drunken way.

"So, you lied to everyone. What else have you lied about?"

"A lot of things," he said and started to blubber. "God doesn't like me anymore."

"You're drunk, Rodney. Tell me the truth. What else haven't you told me?"

"A lot of people hate me. I hate myself sometimes, when I've had too much to drink."

I steeled myself, but asked the question, "Did you have Stephen killed?"

He shook his head violently and crawled toward me. "No! No! You know that. But I think I know who did."

The conversation was turning on itself and getting weirder by the minute.

"We all know who killed Stephen. I found the murderer. Remember?"

He put his right hand on my left knee and collapsed in a heap between my legs. I was getting really uncomfortable. His proximity to the family jewels broke me out in a sweat.

"Hey boss," I said. "I can have you strung up on sexual harassment charges. Why don't you back off?"

"You don't like me, do you?"

I decided to play along. "I think you're about the best person on this planet. Now, why don't you go back to your room and go to sleep?"

"I know who killed Stephen Cross," he said and his eyes swam in his head.

He was talking nonsense. "Rodney . . . " It was too late. His head dropped between my legs and his eyes closed. "Shit," I said under my breath. "Alone in the house with a pervert." If he had been the right kind of pervert, my mood would have been better.

I extricated my legs from beneath his body and crawled out of bed. I didn't care that I was naked. Rodney was too drunk to care or remember. I put one of my four pillows on the floor, maneuvered him off the bed, and covered him with the heavy bedspread. Soon, he was snoring away and I slipped back under the blankets.

Sometime during the night, Rodney crept out of my room. I didn't hear anything until he knocked precisely at seven. He stuck his head around the door and wished me a good morning, as if nothing had happened. He said he would meet me in an hour in the living room. I drew the curtains back. Low gray clouds spit cold rain, diffusing the light. The day reminded me of drizzly mornings in Boston or New York. The wind cut through me on those days—always a sign of colder weather ahead.

I showered and put on jeans and a black sweatshirt. I grabbed my leather jacket, which I had carried on the plane, and headed to the living room.

Rodney was sitting in front of the television watching network news. He was wearing tan chinos and a white shirt. A blue sweater was slung over his arm.

"Good morning," I said cheerfully. My smile stretched across my face. "How are *we* feeling today?" I wanted the glee in my voice to cover him like honey.

He turned to me and with a voice as flat as western Kansas

said, "I'm sorry about last night, Mr. Harper. I have to watch myself sometimes. As you may have gathered, I like to drink. This habit seems to have gotten a bit worse since the whole Stephen Cross affair."

"Acknowledgment is the first step on the road to recovery," I said.

He smirked and said, "You do have a knack for pissing people off, don't you?"

"Only those I love. Do you mind if I have a seat or do we need to get going?"

"Actually, it's time to leave." He looked at his watch, a gold Movado. He called out toward the kitchen. "Abby, we'll be back in time for lunch. Please serve for three."

The ever-present Abby appeared in the dining room and repeated Rodney's instructions.

Three? Things were looking up. Maybe Tony would be the invited guest again. We walked past Abby and through the expansive kitchen to a door that led to a three-car garage. The black Mercedes I had seen in New York was sheltered comfortably inside. It was buffed to a blistering shine. Next to it sat a navy-blue model of the same type. I assumed it must be Carol's.

"Would you mind driving?" Rodney asked. "I'm feeling a bit off this morning."

"No, not at all," I said, relishing the opportunity to put my New York driver's license to good use—in a Mercedes no less. The last car I had driven was the Chevy I stole in Boston when I went to meet Rodney in New Hampshire.

Rodney punched the garage opener and the extra-wide door slid up. I looked out on the large front lawn and circular driveway and thought about how surreal my world had become. I settled in the driver's seat and Rodney took his place as my passenger. He handed me the keys.

"Before we go," I said, "I have one question."

Rodney looked at me warily.

"You said last night you knew who killed Stephen Cross. What did you mean?"

Rodney sighed. "Sometimes I say things I shouldn't. Sometimes I say things I don't remember—like last night. We all know who killed Stephen Cross, but maybe there's more to the story. After breakfast, I want you and Tony to check out something I've discovered near Lynchburg."

"Okay. Let's get rolling."

I backed the car out of the garage and Rodney pushed a button on the remote and the door glided down. I turned left on the circular drive, wound past the portico, and proceeded down the long drive to the gate. Another remote push and the gate opened. I stopped at the road, unsure of which way to turn.

"Left," Rodney said, sensing my indecision. "Toward town."

I looked both ways and seeing no vehicles, pulled the Mercedes into the right lane near the tree line that bordered the road.

The glass exploded around us in violent pops.

Something warm splashed against my face and I caught sight of Rodney slumping toward the dashboard. I hit the gas pedal and leaned forward. A bullet whizzed past the back of my head and the driver's side glass shattered. Then the tires gave away from the barrage of ammunition and the Mercedes fishtailed on the damp road.

The last thing I saw before I blacked out was the trunk of a large pine veering up in front of us. There was a screech and a crash in slow motion and everything went black. For an instant I woke up, my head resting on the air bag. I don't think I moved, but through the haze, I thought the barrel of a paramilitary-style rifle swung by the fractured window.

But then I could have been dreaming—or dead.

CHAPTER SIX

WHEN I WOKE UP I WAS NAUSEOUS AND LYING IN wet grass behind the car. Two beautiful brown eyes were looking into my face. I squinted and Tony Vargas came into view.

"Don't move," he said. "EMTs are on their way." He was kneeling next to me.

"Someone shot at us," I said, not thinking about how out of it I sounded. Blood was running down the right side of my face.

"About twenty rounds," Tony said. "High magazine clip. The right side of the car is like Swiss cheese."

"Where's Rodney?"

Tony pointed toward something I couldn't see. "Dead. Two bullets to the head."

That jolted me awake. I lifted myself up on my elbows.

"Take it easy," Tony said. "You're cut up pretty bad on the right side of your face. I don't think you've been hit. Maybe a concussion."

I looked to my left. A woman was standing next to a man

sprawled in the overgrown grass and dead weeds. I could only see the soles of Rodney's shoes.

"Abby," Tony called out. "Don't make yourself sick."

"Oh, give me a break. I've seen worse," Abby said. "The wounds are pretty clean."

I must have looked incredulous because Tony said, "Abby's my sister. She works with me. Rodney thought he was getting two for the price of one. I was paying her on the Q-T to keep an eye on him. She heard the shots and the crash."

"Two private dicks on a prick," I said and immediately regretted it.

"Yeah, and one of them cooks." Tony laughed and then turned solemn. "No love lost on Jessup. About a million people wanted him dead. I guess our jobs are over now. Glad I got paid a week in advance." He rose up and he looked like Gargantua hovering over me. "I feel sorry for his wife and kids, though. They're going to take it hard."

Rodney's wife, Carol Kingman Jessup, was the icy blonde I met in New Hampshire, along with Janice Carpenter, Rodney's PR rep. I remembered Carol as being very pretty and very reserved. She was a master at "if-looks-could-kill."

Sirens blared down the road and soon a few hunky EMTs were bending over me, asking me where it hurt. I was tempted to tell one in particular that my crotch throbbed, so I must not have been hurt too badly. One took my blood pressure, one studied the wounds on my face, another amused himself by examining my lower legs and thighs for possible fractures.

"You're going to the hospital to get cleaned up," Tony said. "Then every law enforcement officer in the county is going to question you. Probably the FBI, too. Depends on who gets involved. I'd prefer it if all this stayed local and the Feds stayed away."

"And what about you?" I asked. "Are you beyond the veil of suspicion?"

Tony grinned. "Rodney paid my salary. Why would I want to kill him? Besides, I'm an ex-cop."

"They're the worst," I said. "Remind me to tell you my horror stories about cops."

A couple of the EMTs brought over a stretcher.

"No thanks, guys," I said. "I can walk on my own power." The hot one looked at me askance, but I insisted I was all right. "I'll sign the waiver."

I got to my feet and my head swam a little. My legs seemed a bit unsteady, but I made it to the ambulance. I took a seat on the padded cushion inside and the looker crawled in next to me.

"Have fun," Tony said, as he closed the doors. "See you later."

"I'm looking forward to it. Seeing you, that is."

He waved at me as the vehicle sped off down the road, sirens blaring.

Tony was right.

Every Tom, Dick, and Harry cop in western Virginia talked to me. But first, a trip to the hospital, a short drive away, was in order. The visit was perfunctory—a pretty nurse asking me if I could see and hear, or if I was dizzy. I guess she asked the questions because I kept holding on to my head. The magnifying glass came out to see if pieces of glass were embedded in my skin. She took a few slivers out with tweezers. After a few swabs of peroxide, antibiotic cream, and a bandage session, I was out the door, but an hour and a half had slipped by.

A couple of cops stood by their shiny patrol car, waiting to hustle me to the police station. They both had name badges on, but I had no intention of wedding myself to Virginia police so I made up some suitable monikers.

Billie Bob, with the superior paunch that hung over his bulging belted waistline, shuffled me down a miserable hall. The lovely fluorescent lighting did nothing to accent my skin tone or my swathed face. I looked like the mummy in half drag.

Billie led me to an interrogation room that resembled a holding cell. A green metal door with a combination lock and chicken-wired window blocked the way to my personal Shangri-la. The room was furnished with the requisite round vinyl table and black plastic chairs. Surprise! Two other cops waited inside. I hated to reinforce the "good ole boy" stereotype, but all the cops in the room looked as if they had spent a good deal of their time in fast-food restaurants scarfing down greasy burgers and fries. Billie Bob pointed to the one empty chair and I slid into it. I was about as comfortable as a cat on a diving board. They stared. They were checking me out, as wary of me as I was of them. I wondered what they would think of Desdemona. They viewed me as an oddity, a distraction, a snotty New Yorker who stuck his nose in a shit-pile and got more than brown nostrils, to stretch a metaphor. My inquisitors seemed mostly benign, but they weren't waving their pom-poms at a Pride Parade either.

Billie chewed on his pencil and eyed me uneasily. A lazy smile spread across his face. He bit into the yellow wood one last time and withdrew it from his mouth with a slurp. The first question was coming. God, cops made me nervous. I held up my hand and Billie stopped before he could get out a word, his mouth half opened.

"Can I smoke?" I asked. There was no ashtray on the table. Billie Bob nodded at Jimmie Ray and the second cop got on the phone and called someone in the building. To be fair, the cop that arrived with the glass ashtray looked like he was about eighteen and a member of the high school track team. I gave him the once-over. He bolted from the room.

Billie Bob was about to speak again when I held up my hand a second time. "Can I bum a cigarette?"

"Good Christ," Billie said. "You want me to smoke it for you, too?"

Hardy har har.

I rolled my eyes and relaxed in my chair. Jimmie Ray obliged by pulling a pack of Marlboros from his shirt pocket.

"Light, too?"

Billie sighed as Jimmie lit my fag.

"Okay, can we get started now?" Billie asked. "Are you all comfy?" He slurred the question as if mimicking a Southern drawl. Maybe the hick had worn off these guys. I decided not to push my luck.

"First off, why were you driving Rodney Jessup's car?" Billie asked. He rested his pencil, poised to write on a white pad of paper.

I took a drag, inhaled deeply, and blew the smoke toward the corner. "We were going to breakfast."

Billie scowled. "Can I get a little more than that? You New Yorkers do know how to talk don't you?"

"Guess you've seen my DL," I said.

"We know a hell of a lot more about you than you think!" Jimmie Ray chimed in.

I had no intention of telling them about the "something" that Rodney had discovered near Lynchburg. As far as I was concerned, everything that went down in this room was going to be strictly Rodney's confidential business. He was my employer, after all, and I had two hundred and fifty grand to prove it.

"We were going to breakfast and then back to the house to discuss his personal protection. Ask Tony Vargas."

Billie Bob clucked. "Think you did a good job?" Jimmie Ray chuckled.

I was tempted to say, *"I don't give a rat's ass what you think,"* but I kept my mouth shut.

The door opened and the track star entered with a "suit." The track star bolted again, and the suit leaned against the wall. He was slickly dressed in black tailored clothes and a gold tie. He was the brick shithouse type—with a broad chest and thick legs. He opened his jacket and sported his shield.

"Waters," he said calmly. "FBI. Just here to observe."

Billie Bob, Jimmie Ray, and the third cop, Cyrus, gave the suit a look and then turned their attention to me.

Cyrus, another large cop with squinty eyes, spoke up for the first time. "How come two fags are working for Rodney Jessup?"

The question caught me off guard because I wasn't sure of Tony's reputation in town. Coming out is nobody's business but their own, unless they wield power over a defenseless individual, or they make laws that harm others of like persuasion. I resisted the temptation to punch Cyrus's face.

Waters pushed himself away from the wall. "Anthony Vargas is a friend of mine. He's a good man and a fine investigator."

I was thankful for Waters's endorsement of Tony, but I could feel the hate spread around the room like a plague.

"Whatever," Cyrus said and then clammed up.

"All right," Billie said. "Just tell us what happened."

I relayed the story—as much of it as I could without throwing myself or Tony into jeopardy—how Rodney hired me, my trip to the house, and my short time with him and Tony.

Billie Bob seemed satisfied, but I never quite got over the feeling in the room that I might be a suspect in Rodney's killing. I was certain they were trying to peg me as the accomplice to the hit man.

Waters walked behind my chair. "You know who Cody Harper is, don't you?" He seemed proud of the question from the tone of his voice.

"Think so," Billie Bob said. He moved his notepad and lifted a file the paper had been hiding. His eyes narrowed in that "I've got you by the balls" way. Billie flipped through a couple of pages, nodding his head before he spoke. "Drug time, fleeing the scene—later dropped—small-time hustler, suspected connection to a cop's suicide, likes to *dress up.*" He threw the file on the table. "All-round nice guy. Runs with a good crowd."

"That's ancient history," I said. "And the cop killed himself."

"He found the Combat Zone Killer," Waters said.

Looks of approbation around the table were underwhelming.

"He was dead," Jimmie Ray said.

"Yes," Waters countered, "but he found him, which was more than New England law enforcement could do." The suit stepped back to his place near the wall.

A face appeared through the chicken-wire window. I did a double take at first, wondering if my eyes were playing tricks on me. The face was there for only a few seconds and then it was gone. Anthony Vargas. I was sure of it.

Waters nodded his head at me, and then the questions resumed.

My headache continued for most of the day. I saw local, state, and federal police. My cop quota for life had been used up. By the end of my interrogation everyone seemed satisfied that I hadn't killed Rodney Jessup. The onus was now off me and on some unknown suspect. The door finally opened and Cyrus led me down the hall, past the front desk, and to a waiting patrol car in the lot. The surrounding mountains looked like dark lumps in the night. It was chilly outside after 8:30. He smacked on the heater and we took off.

Cyrus had a smaller and less colorful vocabulary than a parrot.

I asked him where we were going.

He only grunted and spit out, "Jessup's."

The gate was open when we arrived at Rodney's. No need for extra security now. The cop stopped under the portico and the residence door opened. Tony stood there, wearing jeans and a black wifebeater. He was holding a Bud. I was sorely tempted to ask him for a beer when I got out of the car, but sobriety extended its siren call as it had so effectively done in the past few years, especially when the chips were down. Cyrus and I dispensed with social pleasantries. The patrol car sped off and Tony and I stood alone at the door.

"Have a rough day at the office, dear?" he asked.

I wanted to smack him, but he was too cute and sexy in the tight jeans and undershirt. Tufts of black hair curled up from under the neckline. As I got closer I noticed he was wearing a linked gold chain, pretty standard for ex-cops.

"Witty," I said, "but you don't know who you're playing with."

"Sorry, I couldn't resist. I've been watching too many *I Love Lucy* reruns."

Lucy. That was a good sign. If he was a Lucille Ball fan, I had him in bed—as good as in the bag.

"Where's Abby?" I asked.

"I gave her the night off. She's been busting her ass for Jessup. All he gave her were orders and a bad case of nerves. Never a compliment."

I flopped down in one of the overstuffed chairs, exhausted from my day. Tony took a seat in a lounger opposite me.

"So, why do we get the house for the night?" I asked.

"Courtesy of Carol. She wants me to stay until she can get here with the kids."

"How long will that be?"

"Tomorrow. They were on a cruise, but they should be in by late afternoon."

"Well, how will we amuse ourselves this evening?"

"Maybe you can tell me why you hate cops." He sipped his beer. "By the way, I do know quite a bit about you. You don't drink. You smoke more than you should. You used to hustle in New York. Did drugs. Sold some coke to make money. Sounds like a hard life."

"That's the abbreviated version."

"Talk," he said.

He crossed his legs and leaned back in the lounge chair. I thought the buttons on my jeans were going to burst open. He put the beer on a side table and folded his arms over his chest. His biceps bulged along with other areas of his body. Sitting in my chair and watching Tony was like being in an old James Bond movie. I was Dr. No, Goldfinger, Largo, or Blofeld admiring my captured spy. His good looks were nearly swallowed by the darkness beyond the huge picture window, but I could see every detail of his body clearly. I could feel his beating heart pounding against mine.

"You give orders, too," I said. "There's only room for one top in this house."

Tony arched an eyebrow and shot me a casual smile. "You move fast don't you, Mr. Harper."

"Only if I know there might be a mutual understanding."

"Why do you hate cops?"

I arched an eyebrow. "Speaking of . . . Who is the fed dick, 'Waters,' and what's he to you?"

Tony fingered the beer can and looked thoughtfully in my direction. "A friend—nothing more. I've known him for a few years. He almost got me into Quantico, but I changed my mind."

I nodded. "Sounds innocent enough."

"He's straight. Got a wife and three kids."

"Am I imagining things, or were you at the police station?"

"Just making sure you were okay. I sent Waters there to help keep the peace. Never know what can happen around here."

"So you sent him around to keep the cops from hammering me?"

"In a manner of speaking."

"That's the reason I hate cops." Tony listened for the better part of two hours while I filled him in on my dreary past, including my distaste for the former Boston police detective Chris Spinetti. I watched him the whole time, judging his reactions, except when

I stepped out in the backyard to smoke a couple of cigarettes. He was engrossed by my story, and although he had another beer, he never acted like he was bored or wanted to drift off to sleep. He appeared to be genuinely interested in my tale of woe, and, frankly, quite impressed that I had overcome it.

"Now, it's your turn," I said.

Tony looked at his watch. "Much too late. I need to get to bed."

"Where are you sleeping?"

"In a guest bedroom. You know where yours is."

He might as well have thrown cold water in my face.

I yawned and said, "I guess you're right."

He got off the lounge and walked toward me. "Let me look at your face."

The right side was covered in bandages, but the bleeding had stopped long ago. I had a purple robin's-egg-sized bump on my forehead that hurt more than the cuts. "The friendly local doctors and nurses say I'm going to be fine. They expect all my organs to make a full recovery."

"I'm sure," Tony said. He gently touched the side of my face and then backed away. "Good night, Cody."

"Good night." I wasn't about to let him get away so easily. "Two questions before you turn in."

"Shoot."

"Rodney mentioned that he wanted us to go someplace today. He didn't say what the destination was, just that it was near Lynchburg. Any idea what that was about?"

"Nope."

"Okay, second question. Are you gay?"

His lips parted in a sexy smile. "I never mix pleasure with business." He turned and walked toward his bedroom.

I, on the other hand, had never had any prohibition about mixing business and pleasure. I hardly knew what the man was talking about. However, I knew that it might take me a while to fall asleep, and, knowing that, I might have to take matters in hand.

I wouldn't try the Jessup trick of sneaking into someone's bedroom. Even I had standards.

I drifted out of bed about eight thirty and took a leisurely hot shower and changed the bandages on my face. When I opened my door, I heard voices in the dining room. Abby and Tony were sitting at the long table enjoying Danishes and coffee.

Abby waved and pointed to one of the six empty chairs. I took a seat next to Tony.

"I made coffee and I can whip up some bacon and eggs, if you'd like," Abby said.

I was suddenly starving, and it had been ages since I'd had a good old-fashioned breakfast.

She poured me a cup of coffee and retreated to the kitchen.

Tony looked smart in blue dress pants and a white cotton shirt. He turned to me, and I shivered with a little electric jolt.

"Sleep well?" he asked.

"Fine, except when I moved my head. This bump hurts like hell." I grabbed a cinnamon bun covered in pecans and glazed frosting and put it on my plate. "Rodney's an even better host when he's—"

I stopped. I didn't want to drive Jessup too far into the ground. After all, he couldn't fight back. Or could he?

"Yeah, I know. The pressure's off from Rodney, but it may be on from Carol."

I cut into the bun, glaze dripping down its side, and put it in my mouth.

Between chews, I said, "Do you think Carol had anything to do with this? She may want to keep you on the case, but I'm sure she has no use for me. The one and only time we met I was in drag."

Tony chuckled. "Must have been entertaining."

"It was the evening after Stephen Cross disappeared. I had to infiltrate the ranks, so to speak. Carol and Janice Carpenter were not amused. Rodney actually took it better than both of them. Of course, he tried to convert me to a religious heterosexual on the spot. 'Hate the sin, love the sinner,' you know."

"Obviously, he didn't succeed."

"Har har. One of his many failings. You didn't answer my question."

"Oh, that." Tony sipped his coffee. "Why don't you ask her this afternoon if she had anything to do with her husband's murder? What do you think she'll say? She and the kids are arriving about three. I think she's in shock. Ever since Rodney was implicated in the Boston business, her life has been turned upside down. Nothing that I've uncovered, which isn't much, has pointed in her direction. I think she's been treading water in this relationship for years."

"When you two showed up at my apartment, he said Carol and the kids were in danger, too."

Abby returned from the kitchen with three steaming plates of food. She must have been a waitress in a previous life because the dishes were balanced perfectly on her arms. She could get a job at Han's if PI work didn't pan out.

"You make quite a ruckus when you demolish a Mercedes, Mr. Harper," Abby said as she sat down.

I dug into the bacon, eggs, and hash browns like a guy who hadn't seen food in twenty-four hours. Come to think of it, I hadn't seen much at all since Jessup's murder, except a dinky hamburger the cops threw at me during questioning.

"Please, call me Cody, or Des at the very least." I shoveled in some breakfast. "Excellent scrambled eggs. Cooked to perfection. So you heard the shots and the crash?"

"The kitchen's on the front of the house. It sounded like firecrackers and then I heard a big metallic thud and glass cracking.

It took me a while to run down there, but I found you both in the car."

"Did you see anything?" I asked.

Tony shook his head. "I think the bump has addled your brain, Cody. Of course not. I would have told you if Abby had. Don't ask about the security cameras. The road is out of range."

Abby lifted her coffee cup. "I think whoever killed Rodney took off through the woods, which makes me think that we're not dealing with an average Joe here. There's a rural road on the other side of the hill—perfect getaway route. I'd say this guy is more than an amateur. He knows what he's doing. He's used to skating on the edge. Maybe a survivalist type."

"A man?" I asked. "Not a woman?"

"Just my gut," Abby replied.

I liked her way of thinking. My first thought was of Carl Roy and his bunch at Aryan America.

"I think you're on the right track, Abby. I could swear I saw an assault rifle before I blacked out, but I can't be sure. Maybe we take a look-see at the other road this morning."

"M16A2?" Tony asked.

The letters and numbers didn't mean anything to me. "What?"

"Military assault rifle used since the 1980s," Tony said. "I'll show you a picture. I don't think we'll find much at the road, but it's worth checking out." He took a piece of paper that was tucked under the right side of his plate and placed it in front of mine. It was a page from a desk calendar.

"Abby and I checked out Rodney's office this morning," Tony said. "His desk lamp was still on. We couldn't get into the drawers because they're locked and the keys are still with Rodney at the morgue. But this must be the Lynchburg connection Rodney told you about."

The date was several days ago. Rodney had written one word in black ink. *Ralston's.*

"Rodney has plenty of phone books in his office, including one for Lynchburg," Tony said. "Ralston's is a shooting range north of town."

"Now we're getting somewhere," I said.

Abby stayed at the house while Tony and I took off for Lynchburg. We decided to check out the other side of the hill after we got back. Lynchburg was about thirty miles from Rodney's home, as the crow flew, but a little farther by road. Tony had taken the remotes out of the Mercedes before it was towed off and had parked his used Crown Vic in the garage next to Carol's car. As we drove away I told Tony about the cassette tape I had received at Han's. He didn't seem overly concerned, although thinking about the voice on the tape and the shooting made me want to duck when we turned out on the road.

"I think he got the fish he was after," Tony said as I fidgeted in the seat and eyed the woods suspiciously.

I was pretty good with directions, so I could tell that we were traveling southeast toward Lynchburg. The spitting rain had stopped overnight, but the sky was still overcast with high gray clouds whose bottoms looked like fuzzy cotton balls. The sun popped out once in a while through breaks in the ceiling.

The Vic roared along in its loosey-goosey manner. I patted the dashboard and waited for Tony to initiate a conversation, but he seemed absorbed in his driving. We traveled through a rolling countryside dotted with homes and farms.

"You never told me about yourself," I finally said.

I still hoped to get to the bottom of the gay question. Instinct told me I was on the right track.

Tony kept his eyes on the road. "Not much to tell, really. The family's from Mexico City. We still have relatives there. My parents immigrated to Phoenix, and I was born shortly after. Abby came along two years later. My dad worked as a security officer for a bank. He was killed in a shootout. That left me in charge of the house, taking care of Mom and Abby." He took his eyes off the road briefly and looked at me. "Had enough?"

"No," I said, and I meant it. I was getting to like this guy more and more and not just from the crotch perspective.

"Glutton for punishment," he said. "I served a few years in the army—just missed Kuwait. Came back, went to school for a time at Virginia Tech. Did some police work and then became a private investigator. I couldn't stand the bullshit in law enforcement. My sister left Mom in Phoenix and came to Virginia to join me in my business. I tried to talk her out of it, but . . . "

"I think she's got the knack. Must run in the family. How did you meet Jessup?"

A smile arose on his handsome profile.

"Nothing glamorous, if that's what you're thinking. I worked for the cops in Buena Vista for a year. I guess I was drawn to the town because of its Spanish name. Rodney Jessup was always well known around western Virginia. I hadn't heard of him before I moved here, but when I finally met him, I realized what a big deal people thought he was. When he was looking for a PI he came to me. Had nothing to do with religion. I'm Catholic."

"There's enough investigative work around here?"

Tony laughed. "Plenty. You live in New York City. You've seen it all. Believe me, everything that goes on in New York goes on in a small town. You name it—murder, suicide, drug dealing, adultery, kidnapping, extortion. The country is crawling with creeps. Most of the stuff I do is pretty standard—divorce, disappearances. In fact, Abby and I have been thinking about moving up in the world. Maybe to a bigger city."

It was my turn to smile. "New York, perhaps?"

"Wasn't exactly what we had in mind. Richmond, maybe."

I sighed. I could not see myself living in Richmond no matter how good looking the man. I wanted to tell Tony that I had some dreams of my own about PI work, but I didn't want to get into the nasty details about how Chris Spinetti had sworn to make my life a living hell if I ever tried. But Chris was out of the picture and maybe it was time to start thinking seriously about a career change. Norm was nice and Han's was what I needed for a rest and a change, but spending my life washing dishes? No way.

The Lynchburg skyline appeared on the horizon between hills. It was bigger than I thought. The shooting range couldn't be far.

"Why did you leave the local police department?" I asked.

"Short story. Longer psychological evaluation. Let's just say it wasn't a comfortable fit."

"Well, all this history has been great," I said, "but let's cut to the chase. About this gay thing?"

Tony turned to me and this time his brown eyes smoked in a controlled burn. "Would you let that drop? You're like a broken record. If I was gay—and I'm not saying I am—I wouldn't want a man to push me into a relationship."

"Okay, I can take a hint. You can't fault a guy for trying." I definitely needed to back off, but I wondered if I didn't have another closeted cop on my hands. They were always trouble.

"Ralston's should be just up the road," Tony said. Clearly, he wanted to change the subject.

The range was busy. The lot was filled with pickup trucks and sedans and we heard the muffled shots inside and the louder reports from the outside gallery.

We got out of the Crown Vic and walked to the locked entrance, a gray metal door with a small window secured by robbery bars. The door buzzed and the lock clicked. Tony opened it and we stepped inside.

Contrary to my expectations, the man in charge, a decent-looking guy in his midforties, was no beer-swilling redneck. He was wearing a dark blue logo shirt with the initials RM in script below the name. I assumed RM stood for Range Master and not the man's name. In back of the RM, behind three-inch thick Plexiglas and under lock and key, were an assortment of pistols and rifles for rent for the unarmed customer. The muffled reports from the indoor range echoed up front.

"Can I help you gents?" the man said.

Tony introduced himself and pulled out his credentials. RM's eyes flicked nervously.

"I'd like to get some information regarding anyone who might be shooting here with a military assault weapon," Tony said.

RM looked at Tony and then at me, focusing on the bandages on the right side of my head, and then said, "Our customer information is private."

"I understand," Tony said, "but perhaps you could—"

"You'd have to get a subpoena or search warrant for that." RM wouldn't budge.

"This is regarding the murder of Rodney Jessup," Tony said. "The gentleman with me was driving Jessup's car when he was killed."

RM's eyes widened and then softened a bit. "I heard about it right after it happened. A shame. I liked Reverend Jessup. I was going to vote for him. He must have been set up; he was such a good man."

I fought the inclination to stick my fingers in my mouth. "Any information you could provide might help us find his killer," I said.

Tony gave me a "shut up" look and said, "Even the past month of your sign-in logs would be useful."

RM smiled slightly. "I guess I could do that. You can look at it over here—out of the way." He slid the bound book, which had been open in front of us, down the counter.

Tony and I scanned the names, about two hundred and fifty of them. Tony even went back an extra month, but we agreed none of the names meant anything to either of us.

Tony returned the book, handed RM his business card, and thanked him for his time. "If anyone is practicing with a M16A2, would you please let me know?"

"We're real touchy about that," RM said, "with the federal ban in place."

"I understand, just let me know if you see anything," Tony said. "By the way, are you the owner?"

"A co-owner," RM said.

Tony shook his hand and we left.

On the way to the car, I said, "You've got a nice, soft touch. You got what you wanted without forcing it."

Tony smiled. "That's usually the way I am."

"I would have stolen the book when he wasn't looking."

"That's the difference between you and me," he said. "Brains versus criminal behavior."

"I don't think that's a compliment." I stopped at the car and pulled out my cigarettes. "Do you mind if I smoke before we head back chez Jessup?"

Tony shrugged. I lit up.

"Why would Rodney Jessup have Ralston's written on his calendar?" I asked. "What did he know that we don't? He was going to fill us in at breakfast."

"Rodney was spooked," Tony said and then looked back at the range office. "Something else bothers me. If he's the co-owner, he doesn't see every customer who comes in. We'd need to interview the other co-owner and all the employees to get anywhere. I think he pushed the book over so we would be out of security camera range. He was trying to hide his actions as best he could."

I pointed to the camera above the door. "They have video of everyone who comes in here. Who knows how long they keep it. Maybe our guy inside knows more than he's telling, but doesn't want to rat on a good customer. One who might be doing something illegal regarding the ban. It would look bad for the range."

"Could be."

"This fag tastes like shit," I said. "What is it—the Virginia air? Pretty soon you'll have me off cigarettes." I crushed it out on the pavement.

Tony smiled. "Good."

"You'll have a harder time breaking me of another habit I have—one that has to do with whips."

"Get in the car. We've got a crime scene to investigate."

"Yes, Master," I said and got into the Crown Vic.

Tony shook his head. "I can't believe you. You don't take no for an answer."

"You're right."

I would get him in the sack yet.

CHAPTER SEVEN

WHEN WE GOT BACK TO RODNEY'S IT WAS ALMOST lunchtime. Abby had made sandwiches, which we wolfed down. We piled into the Crown Vic and headed to the other side of the hill, all of us on edge when we swung out where Rodney was gunned down.

The road Abby had mentioned at breakfast was more of an access path for hunters than anything else. It was rocky and ill defined. There were no clear tracks, although it looked as if someone had driven a motorcycle up the trail recently. I thought it was fresh, not even a day old. Tony thought the same. How many motorcycles were there in western Virginia? We seemed to be getting nowhere at warp speed. I looked at my watch. It was almost one p.m. Carol and the kids were expected at the house in another two hours. Not a pleasant thing to think about. I didn't even know where I'd be sleeping tonight. Carol was sure to kick me out. Oh well, at least I now had enough of her money to pay for a motel.

"Do we have time to walk the hill?" I asked.

"If we hurry our butts along," Abby said. "We better damn well be at the house when Carol arrives. She's more of a hard-ass than Rodney ever was."

I appreciated Abby's assessments more and more.

Tony parked the Crown Vic near the highway and then we walked down the road. The path led into the woods, then it split. Obviously, hunters needed more than one trail for whatever they were after here. Deer? Turkeys? Bear?

When we came to the fork, I decided to take the right side. Abby and Tony took the left. We promised to return to the same location in forty-five minutes. As we walked away, a thought came into my head. "Is it hunting season?" I called out.

"Archery and firearms," Tony said.

"You're shitting me, right?"

"No," Abby said.

"We don't have hunter's vests. We could get killed."

"Make lots of noise," Tony said. "Sing something. No one will confuse you for a deer. Good thing you're not wearing brown."

"Thanks for nothing. I'll have to figure out what I want to sing. Some show tune, I suppose." I scowled. "By the way, I never wear brown."

They laughed and I struck off into the woods. It wasn't hard to make noise. I purposely stepped on dead branches, snapping as many of them as I could. I picked up a hefty downed limb and struck it against tree trunks as I walked. As noisy as I was, there wouldn't be a deer within a mile of me. I tried not to distract myself so much I'd miss something important. I started thinking about what to sing—a number from *Carousel, Cabaret, Annie?* I decided on "My Friends" from *Sweeney Todd*, a beautiful ode to straight-edge razors as instruments of death. The woods were soon filled with the sound of my not-so-Broadway voice.

The hill rose upward quickly and the climbing got a bit rougher. I soon realized my level walking courses in Manhattan had not prepared me for the rocky terrain of the Virginia wilderness. And this hill, or small mountain, wasn't that big. I huffed and hoisted myself past a large hickory tree as I neared the crest. At the top, I found myself in a grove of tall naked oaks surrounded by pines. It was like standing in a cathedral and the silence was overwhelming. The absence of sound reminded me of that frigid winter day in New Hampshire when I found Stephen Cross, his body encrusted in snow. I shivered at the thought of that day, the blinding whiteness, tragedy, and tears. Finding him drained me so much I could barely walk down the mountain. I had to call John Dresser, his boyfriend. I could barely get out the word "Hello," before I broke down.

I rested against one of the large trunks and listened for anything. There was nothing but the infrequent distant rumble of a car, probably from the road that ran in front of Jessup's home.

I looked down the hill. A brush of sunlight split the air between the trees and an ethereal ballet of dust motes danced in the air. The flitting bits disappeared as quickly as they had appeared when the sun drifted behind the clouds. *What am I looking for?* I hadn't noticed any freshly broken tree branches—telltale signs that someone had traveled this way. Nothing, no shiny bullet casings or anything else, glinted up at me from the ground. Not even a boot print. I was indeed looking for the proverbial needle in a haystack.

Standing there, I got paranoid. I began imagining things and expected to hear a bullet or arrow whiz by my head, but quiet prevailed. I walked down the slope a few hundred yards and found nothing. I had to get back soon, so I started up the hill. That was when I noticed the note, facing the direction of Jessup's home, tacked to a trunk. It was a plain piece of blue-ruled school paper, like any sixth grader would have in class, anchored with a red thumbtack.

It read: *I want the kids.*

* * *

"Ruthie and John," Tony said as he settled on the couch with coffee in one hand.

"Who is this guy? Why is he playing games?" Abby asked. "He's one dangerous motherfucker." Her face flushed red after the word came out.

"Don't worry," I assured her. "I've heard the word before. Something about investigative work brings out the potty mouth."

"This means the kids have to be under watch twenty-four hours a day," Tony said. "Carol is going to freak out. What bothers me is that the note was probably placed there this morning. The cops would have found it yesterday if it had been there."

"The note wasn't wet so it couldn't have been left there yesterday," I said. "Do you think those motorcycle tracks were from a particular bike?"

"I'm no expert," Tony said, "but they looked like off-road tires to me. They seemed bigger than usual. Maybe a dirt bike. What do you think Abby?"

She nodded.

"It's as if he anticipates our every move," I said. "Scary."

I had taken the note and thumbtack off the tree by using dead leaves as a makeshift glove, in case there were any fingerprints to be found. When we got home we carefully laid the note out on the coffee table, as if staring at it was going to give us some insight into the mind of the killer.

"This guy killed Rodney for revenge," I said. "We don't know why, but we do know this wasn't a random murder. Now, if I had to guess, I'd say he wants the kids for an exchange of money, or blackmail leverage—some kind of ransom. I don't think he wants to kill them."

Abby nodded. "We have to let Carol in on this. She's got to know her children are in danger."

"They're adopted aren't they?" I asked. "I seem to remember

Rodney telling me about them when we were having our little tête-à-tête in New Hampshire. Orphans from a fire or something?"

"Good memory," Tony said. "Yes, they're adopted. They were orphaned when their parents were killed in a fire in South Carolina four years ago. John was three and Ruthie was only a year old."

"Rodney told me the press had a field day with him when they adopted the kids, as if the adoption was some kind of religious grandstanding to make him look good."

"The more I learn about Rodney," Tony said, "the more I realize he needed religion to make him look good. He was a seriously flawed individual."

I laughed at Tony's diagnosis. "No shit." A thought bubbled into my head. "You know, not one of us seems to have been too broken up about Rodney's death because he was such an asshole, but I feel sorry for the kids."

Abby agreed. We had to consider what we were dealing with. I looked at my watch. It was going on four p.m. We were discussing the next steps to take when the front door opened. None of us had heard a car pull up.

Carol Kingman Jessup ushered Ruthie and John into the hall. From across the room, I could tell she had been crying—her makeup was smeared around her eyes. I assumed she had been to the morgue to identify the body. The three of them looked lost and forlorn, as if they had arrived in the new world from foreign shores. The home they had known for so long must have seemed strange and lonely, occupied by people they barely knew. Tony had told me they had been away for nearly a month.

Carol was still as pretty as I remembered, but her blonde hair looked darker than it was when we last met; her face showed a few more creases around the mouth and eyes. She was wearing a long navy coat and black gloves. She pulled off her gloves and tossed them on the hall credenza. Ruthie and John, both brunettes, walked slowly to the living room. The driver brought their luggage inside. Carol opened her purse and paid the fare for the car service.

When she turned back to us, her eyes narrowed and focused on me.

She scowled. "What's *he* doing here? Or should I say, '*she?*'"

Tony was quick to answer. "*He* was hired by your husband to help track down the person who was threatening him."

"Really?" she said—not in the form of a question, but in a condescending tone that made me feel dirty.

Carol took a pack of filter 100s from her purse and lit up. The smoke breezed past her as she strode into the living room.

"Ruthie, John, go to your rooms. Mommy needs to talk business with the grown-ups."

She waited while the children grabbed their suitcases and headed down the hall. When they were gone, Carol took off her coat and draped it over the couch. "Abby, make me a vodka stinger. On second thought, make it a double. I hope the goddamn drunk didn't sop up all the liquor. I can only *pray* there's some booze left in the house."

I had thought that Carol was the most pious of the lot when I'd had the bad fortune of meeting her the previous summer. My, how the worm had turned . . . .

Abby started to object—resentment blazed in her eyes—but Tony gave her a look that was clear in its message: Play along for a little while longer until the right moment came along to break the news that she wasn't a servant.

Abby skulked off to the kitchen.

The lady of the house drew herself up on the couch like Cruella de Vil. Obviously, I was encroaching in her space, so I excused myself and moved to a chair closer to Tony. She reached into a drawer underneath the coffee table and took out a crystal ashtray. She crossed her legs, placed the ashtray in her lap, and tapped off the ashes.

"At least he didn't smoke all my cigarettes," she said.

I was starting to think Carol should be suspect number one in Rodney's murder. Nothing would have surprised me in this house. I felt sorry for Ruthie and John, and hoped there was plenty of money put aside for their later years—psychotherapy and rehab clinics were expensive. I sat across from Carol, my back to the large picture window. She studied me from head to toe, clearly taking note of the bandages on my face.

"So, who are you again?" Carol asked. She rocked a little on the couch as if she'd already had a drink or two. "You've got some fag drag name."

Tony cringed, but I was more than up for the challenge.

"My *fag drag* name, as you so poetically put it, is Desdemona," I said. "My friends call me Des but don't let that stop you from addressing me by my Christian name, Cody Harper." I wanted to mention the tidy little sum Rodney paid me to get involved in this mess, but thought better of it.

Carol smirked. "Touchy, touchy. There's hardly anything Christian about you." She waved her hand at me before I could reply. "But who am I to cast the first stone?"

She looked around the room and then gazed out upon the darkening lawn. She drew in one last drag of her cigarette before stabbing it out in the ashtray.

"This house hasn't exactly been a Rock of Ages. I think God left quite some time ago. I counted Him absent a while back."

Abby, her eyes like slits and her lips tighter than a one-day surgical lift, came back into the room with the vodka stinger. She placed a white napkin on the coffee table and deposited a large highball glass filled to the rim with the cocktail—vodka and crème de menthe, as I recalled from my drinking days.

Carol reached for the drink, took a gulp, and licked her lips. "You do know how to make a good drink. I think I'll keep you."

"Mrs. Jessup, there's something I think you should know," Tony said.

"No need for formality here," Carol answered. "We're just one big *happy* family. Right? Just one big happy family." She looked into her glass and a loose smile formed on her lips.

"Abby works with me," Tony said. "She and I were working with your husband—"

"Bodyguards? Private investigators? You did a fucking piss-poor job. I know—I saw the body."

"We were on the trail," Tony said. "Cody was driving the car, and could have been killed too. Rodney was going to tell us something he had discovered, but we were too late."

The concrete wall around Carol began to fracture. Tears formed in her eyes. She took a tissue from her purse and swiped at her cheeks.

"I wish I could be sad. I wish I could be sorry that he died, but I can't. That's the part that hurts the most. I really loved him long ago. Then politics took over his life and he changed. Nothing was the same after that." She took another swig of her drink.

Ruthie appeared in the hallway. "Mommy, I'm hungry."

"Just a few more minutes, darling," Carol replied, and she actually sounded civil, as if there was a slim thread of a maternal instinct clinging to her battered soul.

Ruthie turned and walked away.

Tony told Carol about the note I found tacked to the tree. "We don't think it's safe for you and the children to stay in the house," he said. "We all believe a kidnapping attempt is imminent."

"Well, by god, where are we supposed to go? We've been on the run far too long. We've got to stop running sometime."

I asked Carol if I might join her in a smoke. She nodded.

"Someone very dangerous—someone who is familiar with this area and knows what he's doing when it comes to serious weaponry is out there," I said. "He killed your husband and now he's after your kids. Can you think of anyone who would be so intent on destroying your family?"

For an instant, it seemed as though Carol might have had an answer to that question. Something registered in her eyes—a brief flash that seemed to indicate she might know who the killer was. Then the look disappeared as quickly as it had appeared.

"I don't know," she said. "So many people loved Rodney, but so many others had their own reasons to hate him."

"We need a place to start," I said. "Even a name would give us something to go on."

John appeared in the hallway with his sister. "Mom, we're bored. Can we play in the backyard for a little while?"

"No," Carol said. "It's too dark and it's not safe out there."

John's shoulders slumped. "You mean we're prisoners here just like we were on the ship? We can put the yard lights on. Mom, please?"

Carol took another swig of her stinger and said, "I know it's hard to understand, but we have to be careful. You can go outside in the morning."

The kids were about to return to their rooms when Abby said, "I'll go with them so they can get some fresh air. I'm sure we'll be all right."

I knew there was more on Abby's mind than just wanting to go outside. She cared about the kids and wanted to reintroduce some normalcy into their lives to blunt everything else that was going on. It had been a rough afternoon for Ruthie and John knowing they had lost their father. I admired Abby for having the courage to speak up, but I also thought it would have been a better idea for everyone to stay inside for the evening.

"Take my gun," Tony said, and pulled it out from where it was buried under his coat.

Carol gasped.

John's eyes went wide, "Wow, a real gun!" He ran to get a closer look at the weapon.

"This is getting out of hand," Carol said.

Tony helped Abby strap on the semiautomatic. "They'll be okay with my sister," Tony said. "You can watch them from here. Cody and I will rustle something up in the kitchen."

"We will?" I wasn't a whiz in the kitchen but with Tony as my partner I was willing to learn.

"Yes," Tony said. "We have hamburger meat and fixings for tacos."

"How multicultural of us," I said.

Tony shot me that "shut up" look, which he had developed a fondness for doing.

Carol was absorbed in her drink.

Abby and the kids disappeared down the hall toward the bedrooms in the left wing. In a few minutes, they were all out back, coats on, playing kickball on the wide lawn. Underneath the lights, they looked as if they were having fun. Their breaths turned into puffs of steam in the chilly November evening as they ran after the ball.

Tony and I went to the kitchen and began working on the meal. He poured himself a glass of red wine and I grabbed a chilled bottle of water. Tony instructed me to chop onions and soon my tears were flowing.

"So, what do you think?" I asked, wiping away my tears with the back of my hand.

"Carol's scared shitless. Wouldn't you be?"

"I have to admit, I was spooked after Rodney visited me in New York. I kept wondering if someone was going to knock me off. Whoever this guy is, he knows too much." I scraped the onion skins off my knife onto the cutting board. "Where are they going to go?"

"I don't know, but this house is like a bar at closing; 'I don't care where you go, but you can't stay here,' as the saying goes. They *can't* stay here. Do you get the sense that we haven't even scratched the surface with Carol?"

"Definitely. I'm sure the police will want to interview her, too."

We talked as Tony sautéed the onions and hamburger meat and I chopped lettuce. We were getting out the sour cream and salsa, when we heard screams.

And then a shot.

Tony and I ran to the living room and found Carol in hysterics, racing toward the back door. Tony yelled at her to stop.

"Stay here with Carol," I said to Tony as we grabbed hold of her.

Abby was kneeling in the grass, the semiautomatic pointed to the back tree line. The kids were crouched behind her.

I ran down the hall and found the back door. The lights were on timers and there was no way to quickly disable them. I was unarmed, but I opened the door and dropped to the ground. Abby and the kids were about fifty feet away. I crawled, elbow to knee, until I got to them.

Abby was sweeping the trees with the gun.

"I saw this gray and black blur and then a white bag came hurtling out of the darkness," Abby said.

I instructed Ruthie and John to lie flat on the ground. I looked over Abby's shoulder and saw the bag, lying on the far edge of the lawn. "He could have easily done major damage if he'd wanted to. He's trying to make this as excruciating as possible. You fired into the trees?"

"One shot," Abby said, and then added, "I don't think it was a man."

I was astounded that another person might be involved.

"*It* didn't run like a man. I think it was a woman, dressed in camouflage."

I looked back and, through the window, I saw Tony dialing the phone. The police would arrive soon. Carol was huddled on the couch—her hands covering her eyes.

I shielded the kids with my body to get them inside. Abby ran cover, still sweeping the tree line with her gun. We drew the drapes and collapsed in the living room.

Carol was a mess. She hugged Ruthie and John, cried and fussed over them, and then asked me to fix her another drink. I declined, not wanting to enable her habit or get too close to booze even though I did feel sorry for her. Tony relented and fixed her another vodka stinger.

About ten minutes later, three police and two sheriff's patrol cars arrived in the circle drive. There was no mistaking their arrival. One of the officers was in full bomb-squad regalia, holding the leash of a German shepherd sniffer. We didn't see what happened next because we gathered in the kitchen at the front of the house, in case the bag happened to contain explosives. A few officers came inside and questioned Abby. They were all friendly to Tony and his sister. Apparently, the law enforcement brotherhood was tight in Buena Vista tonight.

One tense hour later, an officer showed up at the front door with the mysterious, white bag, holding it delicately in his gloved hands.

"Want to see what's inside?" he asked Tony.

Tony nodded, of course, and the officer pulled the drawstrings on the bag to reveal its contents. Tony peered in and scowled. We were all gathered around the door in anxious anticipation.

"Well, what is it?" I asked.

"Not a bomb," Tony said, with a disturbed look on his face. "It's a naked, rubber baby doll covered in what appears to be blood—or something that's meant to look like blood."

"Not again," Carol said, referring to the pig fetus that had been thrown over the front gate about a month before. She lit a cigarette and said, "That's it—we're getting out of this house as soon as we can. Ruthie, John, don't even bother unpacking."

The kids moaned. I looked at Tony.

"Did you find anything in the woods?" Abby asked the cop.

"Nothing," he said. "We'll come back tomorrow when it's light enough to do a thorough search. I'm leaving now, but a few officers will stick around for a while to make sure you're safe."

"We'll be gone first thing in the morning," Carol said to Tony.

"Where will you go?" I asked. "What about the funeral?"

Carol burst into tears.

"I'll take the kids to their rooms," Abby said. "I think they've had enough excitement before dinner." She enclosed Ruthie and John in her grasp and walked away with them.

"I'm sorry," I said to Carol. "I didn't mean to upset you, but you can't just run out of here without thinking about what to do next."

"Cody's right," Tony said. "You can't go to relatives or friends. That's too obvious. You can't hide out in the area, it's too close-knit a community. Word is bound to get out. We need to put together a plan."

"Where can I go?" Carol asked, brushing away tears.

I'd been thinking about the answer to that question ever since I'd known Carol and the children were coming back to the house.

"New York City," I suggested, as we walked back to the kitchen.

Carol's jaw dropped. "You can't be serious. What are we going to do in New York? Live in a hotel? Or should we just hang out on the street?"

"I'm not being funny. This killer—wants the kids next. That's clear. We need to protect them. I have a friend I would trust with them. I'll be around to guard them, too. That would leave Tony and Abby free to continue their investigation here—paid, of course, for their work."

Carol slammed her fists on the kitchen table. "I'm not leaving my children!"

"In that case, Cody and I will go with Ruthie and John, while you and Abby attend to the funeral," Tony said. "I'm for getting them out of here as soon as possible. The killer seems to be on our heels as much as we try to stay clear."

"Sounds good to me," I said, "and it makes a hell of a lot more sense than staying here."

Carol shook her head. "The funeral's in two days. I have to be here."

"Abby can move you to a motel, under police surveillance," Tony said.

Carol opened her mouth—no doubt to argue—but Tony lifted a hand.

"The first place anyone will check are the more expensive area hotels, you need to stay where no one will think to look for you. Abby can register you under her name. With everything that's going on, I'm sure the police will honor a request for increased protection." He stopped and looked at the hamburger that was still sitting in its own grease in the skillet. "We need to eat. Cody, let's finish cooking. Maybe after dinner everyone will have a clearer head."

Carol walked to the kitchen door and then turned. She inhaled and blew a puff of smoke toward me.

She began slowly as if she wasn't sure what to say. "Cody . . . I'd like to thank you for protecting my kids tonight. They're all I have in the world." She turned and walked away.

Tony looked at me and smiled. "Congratulations, champ. You just won the first bout in a knockout."

The kids enjoyed the dinner and even laughed a bit at my silly jokes. I got the impression they tolerated me because they had never met anyone like me. John appeared to be taking his father's death harder than Ruthie—he seemed more intense during the meal, though it was hard to tell because of his natural childhood resiliency. At any rate, I didn't envy the kids. After all, I was an orphan of sorts—my parents threw me out of the house when I was fifteen for being gay.

After the dishes were cleared, everyone was exhausted and ready for bed. Tony came up with the sleeping arrangements, which suited me. Abby was sleeping on a couch in Rodney and Carol's master suite, while the kids bunked with their mom in the king size bed. One big happy family. The other bedrooms would go empty. Tony and I would be in my guest bedroom on the other side of the house. I couldn't wait.

Tony and I walked from room to room to make sure every lock and window was secured, then we went back to my bedroom. Carol armed the security system before retiring.

Tony said he was going to take a shower. He stepped into the bathroom and closed the door. I decided it would be a good idea for me to shower as well. About fifteen minutes later, he stepped out wearing a towel and nothing else. He put his pants and shirt over a chair. I looked for briefs or boxers, but didn't see any.

I decided it was now or never, what the hell. I left the door open and stripped. The bed was directly across from the shower door, but Tony was nowhere to be seen. I stepped into the shower and luxuriated in the hot, soapy water. I stayed in until my hands began to prune, because the experience of expensive soaps, shampoos, marble tile, and a state-of-the-art showerhead was so unlike my tiny, water-stained New York bathroom, I never wanted to get out.

When I finally opened the shower door, I still couldn't see Tony. Curious, I wrapped a towel around my waist and stepped into the room. He was standing at the window, peering out through a crack in the curtains. His broad shoulders were on display. His deltoids formed a nice V; his waist was trim. I didn't want to interrupt his thoughts, so I pulled down the bedspread, blanket, and sheet, which I had hastily made in the morning. I dropped the towel to the floor and crawled into bed, covering myself with the sheet. I waited there a few minutes until he turned.

My god. I was looking at a dream. His pecs were perfectly formed. A healthy helping of chest hair spread down to his stomach, leading to a treasure trail that disappeared beneath the white towel. His eyes sparkled as he walked toward me. His black hair and light brown skin were set off by the towel. His thighs were meaty under the cloth and an appendage of noticeable size hung between them. My own manhood stirred and I struggled to contain the erection that was rapidly forming. I was fooling myself. Tony noticed and smiled. He pulled the sheet down somewhat coyly and peeked. I was more than willing to oblige.

"Nice," he said. "I've been wondering what it looked like."

He undraped his towel and tossed it on a chair.

Oh god. I had died and gone to heaven.

A furry coating of hair covered his finely cut abdomen and led downward to a thick uncut penis. It stirred under my unflinching gaze.

I rolled on my side toward him and waited.

"Easy there," Tony said. "Don't you think we should get to know each other?"

"Why?"

He got into bed and slid underneath the sheet. "I'm serious."

"So am I."

"Okay, truce. Clearly, there's an attraction. We don't have to act on it tonight—or ever. We're not teenagers."

"Baby, I will have the worst case of blue balls in America if nothing happens tonight," I said. "And, by the way, why so coy with me up until now? And all that beating around the bush about the cops giving you a hard time? No wonder you felt uncomfortable."

"No one ever knew—ha!—and I didn't 'come out.'" He smiled and then looked at me with those eyes. Goose bumps broke out on my arms under his gaze. "I would have if anyone had asked, but I

AN ABSENT GOD

like to take things slow and easy. No need to rush into anything, right? Believe me, I've gone through a lot of shit to get where I am today. I'd rather know I'm doing the right thing, or do nothing at all when it comes to relationships."

"I'm convinced it's the right thing—and tonight's the right night." I reached for him.

"Look, it's been a difficult day." He pulled back. "I don't mind snuggling, but . . . "

"Snuggling it is," I said and wrapped my arms around his shoulders.

A knock on the door interrupted us.

"Who is it? I asked, barely able to hide my irritation.

A small voice whispered outside.

"Who?" I asked again.

"John," came the louder answer. The seven-year-old waited.

"Shit," I whispered to Tony, "get some underwear on." I grabbed some boxers from my bag and Tony pulled on his pants, both erections falling fast. I looked at him.

"I don't like underwear," he said to me.

"You're kidding me, right? Free-balling?"

"Yes," he whispered. "You should talk. We'll compare our lists of vices someday." He pointed to the door. "See what the kid wants."

I held the towel in front of me and opened the door. John, looking as angelic as hell, stood there in his starched pajamas. He looked at the floor with downcast eyes. "Can I sleep with you guys? I don't want to sleep with a bunch of girls."

I looked at Tony. His dreamboat face lit up happily.

"Come in, partner," Tony said. "You can sleep between us. You'll be nice and safe, and so will we."

Crap, I thought. *Foiled by a seven-year-old.*

We all crawled into bed, me in my underwear and Tony in his pants, with John between us.

Tony looked at me and said, "Didn't you ever want to have kids?"

I coughed. "I plead the fifth."

"What's that?" John asked.

"Go to sleep," Tony said. "I'll explain it later. Tomorrow's going to be a long day."

"It's going to be a long night," I said and reached over and turned off the light.

CHAPTER EIGHT

WE ALL MET AT THE BREAKFAST TABLE THE NEXT
morning to make plans. We watched through the big window
in the back as the cops scoured the woods for about an hour.
A couple of them talked to Tony and told him they had found
nothing. They left a short time later.

Carol seemed distracted and distant while we talked about
our best options for protecting the children. I understood what
she must have been thinking: *How the hell did this happen? I'm
sending my kids off to New York City with two men I hardly
know.*

But what other choice did she have? Tony was right. She and
the kids were too well known to stay with relatives or friends.
Sticking close to Abby and asking for police protection was her
best bet at staying alive. At least in New York the kids could
blend in with the millions of other people.

By our last cup of coffee, we had formulated our plan. Tony
and Abby would drive Carol's Mercedes away from the house to
the motel, with Carol and the kids hidden in the backseat. Abby

suggested making it a game for Ruthie and John's sake, which we all agreed was a good idea. No need to scare the kids to death on the day of their father's funeral. Tony would drop the two women off at Abby's apartment to pick up her car and they would proceed to the motel for their stay—however long it took to wrap up Rodney's affairs. While Tony started out for New York in Carol's Mercedes with Ruthie and John, I would take the Crown Vic and follow them to New York, hoping to rendezvous near Harrisburg, Pennsylvania, for a caravan into the city.

We'd all spend at least the night at my apartment before taking the kids to Ophelia Cox's apartment—I didn't tell them that Ophelia was a drag queen. I wanted to bring up another part of the plan, although I figured it might not go over too well. We were about to leave the table when I popped the question.

"Carol, do you have a wig I could borrow? And a nice dress?"

Tony nearly spit out his coffee. Carol and Abby looked at me in amazement. Ruthie laughed and John sniggered.

"Before you all think I'm crazier than I am, consider the brilliance of this plan. We're about the same height." I worded what I wanted to say delicately because I didn't want to scare the kids. "If I leave in the first car, dressed like Carol, I think she'll be safer."

Without missing a beat, Carol said, "I wouldn't be caught dead in that heap you're driving."

"Now wait a minute," Tony said, "don't trash Vicky."

Carol tapped her polished red fingernails on the table. "Oh great, you've named your car. I think I'm the only sane one in this house, besides the kids."

"It's not the car that matters so much—it's the illusion of me being you that would distract someone," I said.

"The whole idea is crazy," Carol said.

"You saw my work in Manchester. You know how good I look."

Carol sighed and then lifted her hands in resignation. "Heaven protect me."

"Well, we should get started," I said. "Beauty doesn't happen in a minute."

As it turned out, Carol had plenty of wigs in her living room–sized closet, and enough dresses to make Cher jealous. She also had enough cosmetics in her bathroom to make any drag queen swoon. Carol threw a few dresses on the bed and gave me permission to do anything I wanted to make them fit. I had to make small slits on both sides, but otherwise the dress I chose was perfect. Fitting into Carol's shoes, on the other hand, was a bit of a challenge; but if the dress was long enough it didn't matter too much. I found some open-backs that worked if I didn't mind my toes being a little cramped.

The transformation took about an hour, so I was the last to walk into the living room, but when I did, the reception was unanimous. The blonde wig, the long-sleeve, calf-length blue dress, and the rudimentary makeup had done the trick.

No, I didn't look exactly like Carol, if you were looking directly at me, but a sniper at one hundred and fifty yards might be hard pressed to tell the difference. He would have to make a split-second decision whether to fire. And the indecision might be enough for me and the others to get away with our lives.

Tony whistled. Carol actually smiled. She and the kids were huddled under a blanket that would serve to hide them in the backseat. I spun around in a broad circle, swinging the black clutch Carol had given me. The whole scene was surreal, as if we were heading, with suitcases in hand, to some bizarre costume party. Tony and Abby checked the house to make sure it was secure before we walked to the garage.

"Good luck everyone," I said and considered that we had an eight– to ten–hour drive before reaching the city. "Tony, you have the directions to my apartment?"

Tony nodded. "I was the one who found—well, you know."

He had driven Rodney to my apartment what seemed like years ago.

I also wanted to make sure we met at a rest stop near Harrisburg. "We'll plan to meet soon. By the time you drop off your sister and Carol, we'll both be on approximately the same timetable."

Tony cocked an eyebrow. "What have you got cooking up that pretty sleeve?"

"Don't mix metaphors. I'm making a quick stop before I get on the interstate. Nothing important."

"I don't believe you," Tony said, raising an eyebrow. "Stay safe."

"Always."

I watched them get into the Mercedes and then I squeezed into the Crown Vic. Carol's dress was a bit tight on me. Tony waved and pushed the remote garage door opener. It slid open and I backed out into the circular driveway. The day was sunny and mild for a change. I parked the car in the driveway and waited for Tony to back out the Mercedes. I planned to turn right at the gate and then circle back. Tony would turn left after I pulled out onto the road.

When both cars were out and the garage door was secured, I started down the lane toward the gate. My heart raced as I neared the wrought-iron metal. What if the sniper lay in waiting? I hoped lightning wouldn't strike twice, but I couldn't be sure.

Tony hit the button for the gate and it swung open. I searched the trees for any sign of movement, but it was like looking into the ocean for a fish. There was nothing to see but tree trunks, naked branches, and evergreens.

I gunned the Crown Vic and turned right, squealing the tires along the way. I ducked as low as I could to stay out of possible gunfire, but nothing happened. Soon, I was five hundred feet or more down the road, well beyond the gate. In the rearview mirror, the Mercedes adopted the same mode of escape, only going the other direction. Tony punched the accelerator and the car roared off toward town. I drove a country mile, then turned around and whizzed past the property. The gate was closed and all was well.

No one knew I was headed to Ralston's.

I drove the same route we had taken the day before. I pushed the hell out of Vicky and arrived in the parking lot in about forty-five minutes. I parked so the car's plates were out of camera range. I checked my makeup in the visor mirror and decided I was presentable enough, certainly not gorgeous. On the other hand, I didn't want to look too beautiful at a shooting range. My lipstick was smeared a bit. I had swiped one of Carol's and put it in the purse. I reapplied and then got out of the car. The shoes were a dead giveaway. I hoped the yokel behind the desk would be so oblivious he wouldn't notice. My hands lacked makeup—another problem. With so much wrong, the guy behind the counter would have to be a total idiot not to notice.

I adjusted my dress and walked to the door. It buzzed open and I stepped inside. The man behind the counter was not the man Tony and I had seen the day before. He was younger, good looking, and wore the same logo shirt, but without the RM initials. He was an early morning shift employee.

He looked at me and smiled. Then he winked. He knew I was a man and it didn't bother him one bit. Considering the fast drag I came up with, I wasn't surprised. Like Carol in the Crown Vic, I wouldn't have been caught dead in New York in the outfit I was wearing.

"Can I help you?" he asked. I could tell he was trying to control his laughter.

I shot him a beat-down stare and flipped the curls on my wig. "I'd like to see you come up with something better in an hour's time." That shut him up. "I need to rent a pistol for practice. That okay with you?"

He got a little more serious and said, "We don't ask for anything from our customers except state issued ID. What kind of gun are you looking for?"

"Glock. Nine millimeter."

"We've got several. Give me a few minutes." He started for the cage to look at the rental guns. As he walked away, I could have sworn he said under his breath, "Must have been a hell of a party. Sorry I wasn't invited."

I needed less than a minute. As he fiddled with the lock, I slipped my hand over the counter where the log-in book had been yesterday and my fingers landed on the cover. I gave it a quick tug and it popped into my left hand. I lifted it and looked. It was the same book Tony and I had pored over. The cutie had disappeared behind a wall. I hiked up my skirt, secured the book between my panty hose and stomach, and walked out the door.

I ran to the car, wrestled the book out, threw it on the seat, and started the ignition. I hightailed it out of the lot. Several cars passed me going the other direction as I sped down the same road I had taken to get there. I kept looking in the rearview mirror to see if the door to Ralston's had opened, but it hadn't. Soon, the highway curved and the building disappeared from sight.

Cutie was probably looking at the videotape now—and calling the police.

The next time I saw Tony he was sitting on the hood of the Mercedes outside my apartment. I hadn't eaten since breakfast and I was hungry as hell. The kids were asleep under the blanket in the back of the car. We had missed each other in Harrisburg and proceeded on our respective ways. I changed clothes during a pit stop in Pennsylvania. Fortunately, no one was in the lot when

I pulled in so I was able to slip out of the dress and wash the makeup off my face.

"I'm dying for a beer," Tony said, as I lit up a cigarette.

"Maybe if we work on it, we can both rid ourselves of our respective vices." I looked at my watch.

It was getting too late to go to Han's for a meal, so I suggested Tony go park the car in a garage on Forty-Fourth Street and I'd dig out a can of soup—or something that was at least nutritious from my small store of canned food.

I reached into the car and tugged on John's shoulder. "Time to get up, sleepyhead."

John's eyes fluttered open and then closed. Ruthie didn't stir.

I looked at Tony. "Isn't that what you're supposed to say? Something cute like 'Time to get up, sleepyhead?'"

Tony laughed. "You need some brushing up on your parenting skills."

"Never had any." I opened the back door of the sedan and lifted Ruthie out of the seat. John sprang awake protectively and started to swing at my arms, but stopped when he saw it was me.

"Don't worry, champ," I said. "You're at your new home." I put Ruthie under my left arm like a bag of potatoes and lifted my right arm like a model on *The Price Is Right*. "All this can be yours." Ruthie was unimpressed, but John's eyes widened when he stepped out on the street and looked north and east toward New York's towering skyscrapers. Tony got the luggage out of the trunk.

"Wow," John said.

I opened the door to my apartment. "You ain't seen nothing yet."

The kids had been composed in their home in Virginia, but they must have thought my apartment was a playground. I'd never seen a brother and sister so happy. Then, I remembered the whips and leather accessories I'd attached to my bedroom wall. I had collected a few here and there over the year; it reminded me of my apartment in Boston that had been emptied by the police during their investigation of the Combat Zone murders. The nice warm smell of cowhide brought an earthy charm to lonely, cold New York City. And although I really hadn't had much use for the objects on the wall, I figured one day I would have to emerge from my monastic cavern.

The kids ran to my semi-reassembled collection of phonograph records piled on the floor. They pulled out a few albums and then ran to my bookcase. John stuck his head in my bedroom and said, "Wow." That seemed to be his word of the day.

"You have whips on the walls," he said. "Do you have a horse? Dad used to take us riding."

"Why don't you have a seat on the couch and read a book," Tony said before I could say something smart. He glanced at the volumes on the shelves and then looked at me. "On second thought—don't you have a television?"

"Not me. Give me a good book any day."

"Yeah, well, I'm going to park the Mercedes in a garage farther away—too obvious on the street with the Virginia plates. What about Vicky?"

"Vicky'll be all right on the street until eight tomorrow morning. We'll have to move her then. But we'll talk about that later." I was thinking of a good time to bring up Ophelia. The Virginia plates on Vicky didn't work in our favor either. A killer who knew where I lived would make the connection that the kids were with me. Another reason to pass the kids to Ophelia.

"Okay, you two, what do you want to eat?" I asked after Tony left.

I opened my small kitchen cabinets and looked inside. There were a few cans of soup, a couple of tins of tuna fish, and some ramen noodles. Nothing too appetizing. I hadn't realized how much I depended on Han's for meals.

John shook his head like he wasn't hungry and Ruthie asked, "What have you got?"

When I told her she shook her head, too.

"We ate at McDonald's about sunset," John said. "It was fun. I liked the Big Mac."

"You've never eaten there before?"

"No," Ruthie said. "Mom and Dad wouldn't let us."

I was beginning to put together the big picture. Pious mom and dad, who both hit the sauce pretty hard, among other questionable habits, kept the kiddies pure and wholesome, apparently so they would have a clear path to heaven. New York was going to be an eye-opening experience for them.

"Well, amuse yourselves while I make some soup. I'd take you to the restaurant where I work, but it's too late. Great Chinese food."

"Wow, I'd love Chinese food," John said.

"Let me guess, you've never had it."

They both nodded.

The only books with pictures I had were a couple of old encyclopedia yearbooks I'd found on the street. I gave them to the kids while I made the soup. I was finishing up when Tony knocked on the door.

"My god," he said. "It's twenty dollars a night to park the car. Highway robbery." He held up a blue receipt ticket.

"That's one of the cheaper spots," I said. "But, don't worry, I'm loaded. Remember? At least for the moment."

"Oh, yeah." He looked at the kids sprawled out on the couch. "What do we do now? Play poker?"

"You're the one with the parenting skills."

"It's just that your apartment is so . . . cozy."

I clapped my hands and Ruthie and John looked at me like trained dogs. "Since you don't want to eat, it's time for bed. Ruthie, you're going to sleep on the couch. John, you're going to bunk on the floor—we'll pull the cushions off the chairs to make it comfortable. We're all going to pretend we're camping. But let's pretend we're in the mountains instead of New York and we have to watch out for lions and tigers and bears. Tony and I will be in there with the door open in case you get scared."

John huffed and threw his book down on the couch. "There aren't any lions and tigers and bears in New York."

"Depends on what you're looking for," I said. Tony scowled. "And, besides, there *are* wild animals in New York City right in Central Park."

"Really?" John asked.

"Really. And if you're good and obey your uncle Cody like you should, you might get to see them."

The kids put away the books and started to get ready for bed.

"One at a time in the bathroom," I said. "Ruthie, you first."

In a half hour, everyone was ready to turn in. The kids were nestled under the blankets. I grabbed an old bedspread I had in my closet and stretched it over the chairs. It made a nifty tent for John, and was exactly the effect I was after. It didn't take long before they were both asleep.

Tony and I finished off the soup and crawled into bed, both of us tired from the long drive. He lay next to me, his arms crossed over his chest like a corpse. I was in my bathrobe. I had given him a pair of sweatpants to get into, although the leg bands stopped about two inches above his ankles. I thought he looked cute, particularly in the way the fabric bunched around his package.

"You're not so bad with the kids," he said. "Nice job."

"Maybe I do have it in me," I said. "I've never thought of being a dad—my experience with my parents wasn't so good." I turned on my side and stroked his arm. "Not many people have asked about my family—not even Stephen Cross. Once, a long time ago, a man in New York City cared enough . . . do you want to know?"

It looked to me like Tony nodded, but his head might have been lolling on the verge of sleep.

"You might as well know now instead of later."

He turned his head toward me.

"My parents kicked me out of the house ten days after I turned fifteen. My dad was, to put it bluntly, a drunk. He claimed he was disabled, and he was, but it was hard drinking that led to his health problems. We went from fairly good times in Westchester to living in a trailer outside of Danbury.

"He was angry at me and at my mother and spent most of his time coping with a depression made worse by the alcohol. He couldn't make a living anymore. He was a washed-up insurance salesman. My mother had to hold the house together, so she pretty much accepted his rage. When I told them I was gay, he exploded. He kicked me out of the house with nothing but the clothes on my back. My mother stood by. Her spirit had been crushed by our miserable lives."

Tony patted my arm. "Horrible. My family was so different."

"I don't tell many people this because the truth isn't pretty. I have enough baggage to deal with without getting sad or disgusted looks from so-called friends. That's why I turned to drugs and other diversions. I was wound tight. No one wanted to listen and, frankly, I didn't want to tell."

Tony edged closer to me. "Go on."

"On day eleven after my fifteenth birthday, I was in Times Square. I'd hitchhiked all night and slept under a bridge for a couple of hours. That morning, I hustled in a porn theater on Forty-Second Street. Oddly enough, he was a businessman from Westchester. At the Pussycat Theater. I got twenty bucks for fifteen minutes' work. Not bad for a starving kid.

"I ate a steak for lunch and the rest is hustler history."

Tony stared at me. "How did you do it?" He lowered his gaze. I knew he regretted the question.

"Come again?"

"I didn't mean it as an insult. I meant how did you survive?"

I turned on my back and settled into the pillow. Note to land-lord: *the ceiling needs painting.* "Believe it or not, there were men and women living in the city who were in worse shape. Bums, beggars, and winos huddled in doorways or subway exits, without a dime to their names and no roof over their heads. I counted myself lucky. At least I could make a living."

"But hustlers wear out," Tony said.

"I know all too well. The charms of the street don't last long. Sex strangled me, but kept me alive. I worked as long as I could until I found other ways to make money. Drugs. Dealing to friends and strangers. Odd jobs."

Tony propped himself up on his elbow. "How did you dig yourself out of it?"

"Something clicked in my head one day. It wasn't like I suddenly regretted everything I'd done. I wanted to do some-thing different; I guess make more of my life. It was the oddest sensation—feeling like I might have more to live for than being a washed-up, drugged-out hustler.

"The miracle didn't happen overnight. I hung around Times Square for a while until I got the flu and ended up at a home for wayward boys on the Lower East Side. An ex-Catholic priest took me in and became my mentor and friend. He was the one who introduced me to the great writers and dramatists."

The books I'd left behind in Boston when I'd been forced to run appeared in my mind's eye. Volumes of Shakespeare, Marlowe, Tennessee Williams, and William Inge. Of all the belongings I lost in Boston, my books meant the most to me. Many times I had teared up thinking about that loss.

"For two years, I wrote, studied, and learned all I could until money ran out for the home and it closed." Anxiety pierced my chest. "I fell off the wagon. Pretty soon, I was back on the street."

Tony yawned.

"Am I boring you?"

"Not at all. I'm just tired from the drive."

"Well, I'll change the subject. History is depressing. I've got something to show you that'll perk you up." I pulled the Ralston's logbook from under my pillow. I had placed it there when Tony was in the bathroom.

His eyes widened. "You hot shit. How did you get this? Like I need to ask."

"I used my feminine wiles."

"But why?"

"A fortune-teller in Boston once told me I had the gift of prophecy. I can't say she was exactly on target, but I do trust my gut. I think this book is important and I think we may have over-looked something."

As he leafed through the pages, I said, "And one other thing."

He rolled his eyes. "Not the gay question again."

"No, I think we confirmed the answer to that. I want the kids to spend their time here with a dear friend of mine."

Tony looked puzzled. "Say again?"

"This apartment is too dangerous. If *you* can find me, a killer can find me, too. And, as you know, someone who didn't want me involved in this in the first place already knows where I work. I think it's safer for the kids to stay with Ophelia."

"Okay."

Tony handed the book to me and started to turn over, but stopped short when I said, "He's a former drag prostitute and heroin addict—and he has AIDS."

He lurched up on both elbows. "Are you crazy? Carol will have a fit. She'd never allow her children to be with—"

I stared at him and his face turned crimson under the velvety brown.

"With what? A drag queen? A gay transvestite? A hustler? An ex-addict? A leper?"

Tony sighed and slumped against his pillow. "Cody, I'm sorry, but I don't think it's a good idea. I know everybody has a history, but . . . "

My body was growing frosty under my robe. The temperature in the room had dropped to an icy level. "I disagree. It's a great idea and there's no finer person in New York City than Ophelia Cox."

"Ophelia Cox?" He shook his head. "You're kidding me, right? Maybe we'd better talk about this in the morning."

"Yeah, maybe, but I assure you I'm not kidding."

I got out of bed and switched off the overhead light. I crawled back in and Tony and I turned away from each other. An iceberg that could sink the *QE2* was between us.

Another long night lay ahead.

The kids ate bagels and cream cheese and drank orange juice I'd purchased at the Korean deli at the end of the block. I'd moved Vicky into the garage as everyone was getting ready and stopped by the deli on the way home. Tony and I sat on the couch eating cereal and arguing quietly. He was convinced the whole idea of sending Ruthie and John to stay with Ophelia was a huge mistake. I was getting irritated with him and during a couple of points in our discussion I had to hold myself back. His arguments seemed ignorant and off base, particularly for a gay man who should know better, but then he didn't know Ophelia like I did. I had been avoiding telling Tony everything about Ophelia because I wasn't sure what his reaction would be, but I knew in my gut that sending the kids there was the right thing to do, not the least of which would be for their safety.

I told him Ophelia was no longer doing drag, turning tricks, or injecting heroin. I reiterated a fact he knew, but some people still couldn't wrap their heads around. AIDS could not be spread by kissing or casual contact. I was sure Robert would love the kids. It would take his mind off his medical troubles. And if he had to work at Club Leo, Tony or I could babysit at the apartment until he got home. I wasn't sure how long Ruthie and John would be with us, but I had a feeling their stay might drag on until Carol decided to move away from Virginia or take another extended vacation.

After breakfast, Tony picked up the phone and called his sister. She and Carol were getting ready to leave for the funeral home. She told Tony that she was fine, but whispered that Carol was a mess. She then put Carol on the phone and the kids told her excitedly about their night camping out in the wilds of New York City. John seemed happy and content once the phone call had ended, but Ruthie sobbed a little when she hung up. John and Tony tried to comfort her without much luck. I picked up a photo book of the city and pointed out the places we might visit. She was fine by the time we finished looking at the pictures.

"Okay, where do you want Uncle Tony to take you today?" I asked.

He shot me a look that would turn frosting sour. "Uncle Tony? Don't we have some work we need to do?"

"What work? In case you didn't notice there are no leads we have to chase. Taking care of our children is our most important task."

Tony smirked. "What idea is cooking in that little brain of yours?"

"I'm going to call the good friend we've talked about *ad nauseam* and see if he will agree to my *little* plan—I need to check in on him anyway. And, I have to go to Han's and see when Norm wants me back at my delicious job. It might be this afternoon."

"Aren't you rich?"

"Yes, but material wealth is transitory. It's a pity, isn't it? It's emotional riches that I crave." I leaned down and whispered in his ear, "And what happens if Carol decides she wants the money back? She might claim that Rodney wasn't in his right mind. I wouldn't rule out a *big* lawsuit. And then where would I be? Up to my Playtex Living Gloves in dirty dishwater."

"You're not giving up on this Ophelia thing are you?"

"No."

"I want to see the wild animals in Central Park," John said.

I turned to him. He had cream cheese spread over his upper lip like a white mustache.

"There you go," I said. "It's settled. Off to see the animals." I opened my wallet and handed Tony forty bucks. "Buy them popcorn and lunch." I lifted the roach motels I'd placed under the kitchen sink and found an extra set of keys I'd buried there. I handed them to Tony.

He took them like he was handling radioactive isotopes. "Thanks so much, Uncle Des."

I patted him on the back. "Keep a close eye on the kids. Carol and Uncle Des are depending on you—and don't lose those keys. They're the only extra set I have."

We got the kids ready and off for the park. I had no idea being a father could be so much work.

The day was cool, but not cold. Tony holstered his gun under his jacket. I followed them down to Times Square, enough distance to make sure they weren't being tailed and then headed back to the apartment. I called Ophelia hoping to get an answer, but the machine kicked on. I looked at my watch. It was about ten thirty. Ophelia probably wasn't up yet.

Although Virginia was a nice change from my usual city crawls, I missed New York and wanted to get outside. My claustrophobic apartment was unsuited for relaxing at home—unless it was dark or rainy and I wanted to settle in. And there were no Central Park views through my basement windows. Taking a trip to Ophelia's was a much better option than sitting around the house. The smoggy New York air would do me good.

I hadn't felt the need to pack the Smith & Wesson .357 in a year, but today I reconsidered. Another gun I'd bought on the cheap at a Times Square pawnshop was gaining favor as my new favorite. I dug them both out from under my bed and decided on the six-inch IMI Desert Eagle. It was lighter than my other gun. Both were unloaded. The shells were on the top shelf of my bedroom closet.

I put on my leather shoulder holster and jacket, gave a quick glance through my windows, and then opened the door. Rodney's murder came rushing back to me and I shivered. The possibilities for getting murdered in New York were endless. How many rooftops, alleys, and cars could a sniper take advantage of? Something else bothered me as well. Tony and I didn't have one strong lead. Murdering Rodney Jessup was like assassinating a political figure—any wacko among the millions out there was suspect. We had to catch a break, otherwise we would be glorified babysitters until Carol picked up the kids or something more tragic happened. The suspicion nagged at me that the solution to Rodney's murder might be simple if we just knew what to look for.

I glanced over my shoulder as I closed the door. I didn't like living my life this way. I'd gotten used to a certain sense of tranquility after the Combat Zone murders. I put the key in my pocket and turned toward the street. Fortunately, I was able to get to the sidewalk, and then to the subway, unscathed. I breathed in the New York City air, that strange mix of exhaust fumes, sewer steam, roasted peanuts, and, depending on which way the wind was blowing, watery smells from the Hudson and East Rivers.

I arrived at Ophelia's apartment in the Lower East Side about thirty minutes later and rang the Martin/Cox buzzer. A sleepy voice crackled through the intercom.

Robert buzzed me in and I took the creaky elevator to the fifth floor. He opened the door and peeked over the chain lock. Seeing me, he let me in. He was dressed in a long, filmy woman's robe, rather like a peignoir, something Liz Taylor or Loretta Young would have worn in the comfort of their homes. His head was as slick as a cue ball after having shaved off all his hair. That look combined with the flowing robe made him look like a bald-headed exotic bird.

His apartment was nice. It faced south and east, so the morning sun warmed the room with its yellow slanted rays. The furniture was okay, certainly nothing fancy. The rooms were clean and sparse and arranged artfully; Zen in their own way.

I sat on the green couch, noting that it could easily fit two kids for sleeping. "How have you been?" I asked.

"All right." His voice was low and gravelly. He sounded lethargic and depressed.

I took out my cigarettes, but he stopped me with a wave of his hand.

"Please don't," he said. "I get enough smoke at the club. I think it's making me sick."

I couldn't argue with that, so I put them back in my pocket.

"I'm losing a lot of weight," he said and then thrust out his arms.

His arms were beginning to take on an emaciated look, mostly bone and thin flesh. "Are you strong enough to work?"

"Yes, but it's a struggle. Most days I'm okay. I just get tired." He looked at me and I felt the specter of death staring at me from the wan face.

"I think you should quit. The job's not good for you."

He laughed and his teeth showed white and skull-like, against his tight lips. "What am I going to live on? My good looks?" Tears formed in his sunken eyes. "I wish I could change the past, but I can't. Now I have to live with this."

"I can lend you what you need."

He leaned forward in his chair and stared at me. "There's a new drug out there, but it's not even approved by the FDA. I heard about it on the street. It's expensive. Someone said it's a thousand dollars a pill."

I was so shocked I didn't know what to say. I wished for the good old days when we were comparing makeup tips and laughing about tricks. Those days were gone. "That has to be a rumor," I said and looked out the window toward the roof across the street.

"Do you know how many friends have dropped me, left my life completely because of this disease? I've been called stupid, irresponsible, and a disgrace because I contracted this nightmare. One of them even told me he wished I'd die and get it over with. Many of them wonder how I could have allowed myself to get AIDS when we've known about it for fifteen years. Those people don't understand anything about addiction."

I was dying for a cigarette. I fidgeted with my belt buckle. "Get as many pills as you need. I'll pay for them."

He sighed and leaned back in his chair. "I can't ask you to do that."

"Yes, you can. I'm your friend—and besides, I'd like you to consider a favor."

He looked at me, puzzled, wondering what strings were attached. I filled him in on the entire story of the Combat Zone murders and then brought him up to date on everything that had transpired since Rodney Jessup had showed up outside my apartment. His eyes shone a little brighter by the time I had finished the story.

"Do you think you're up to it?" I asked. "I don't want you to exhaust yourself. Tony can help out, too."

"Do you think they'll accept me?" Robert asked, apparently without thinking about his condition.

"Ruthie and John are excited about anything new in their lives. Outside of the church and some vacation travel, they've experienced very little. I know they would love it."

He thought for a moment and then said, "I have my good days and my bad days. Mostly, I'm getting by. Maybe the new drugs will help, but, in the meantime, I can't mope around the apartment. I'd love to have them here. They'll keep my mind off my troubles."

I held up my hand. "Before you say yes, consider that Ruthie and John are in danger and that puts you at risk, even though Tony and I are doing everything in our power to make sure nothing happens to these kids."

He looked down at his thin arms. "What have I got to lose? When do you want to bring them over?"

"Tonight, after dinner."

"Good. I'm off today."

We firmed up our plans and I left. I lit up in the elevator on the way down. A gray-haired woman with two shopping bags gave me the finger as I stepped out in the foyer in a haze of smoke. She pointed to the no smoking sign pasted on the elevator's back wall. I shrugged and said I was sorry.

I was struck with a sudden case of nerves. I had a bad feeling and I didn't like it. My gut was turning flip-flops big time. Maybe Tony was right—leaving the kids with Ophelia might be a mistake. But the apartment seemed very secure. People had to be buzzed inside from the lobby unless they had a key. Beyond that, no one would think to look for Ruthie and John here; the assailant would have to know who Martin/Cox was. Ophelia's building was the tallest on the block. The roof across the street was one floor lower, so a sniper would have a harder time hiding, and an even more difficult shot upward instead of down or across. The arrangement made perfect sense, but I had a nagging feeling the murderer knew every step we were taking.

The killer was waiting for the perfect moment.

CHAPTER
NINE

I BROKE THE NEWS ABOUT OPHELIA TO TONY. HE was a little more convinced after a day of babysitting. We hashed out all the reasons again for moving Ruthie and John. Apparently tramping around New York City had worn out the stud and the kids. It was about three p.m. Tony took off his shoes and put his feet up on the couch. Ruthie and John were stretched out on my bed taking a nap. We needed to eat so I thought I'd take the gang to Han's for an early dinner.

"It's got to be something simple we're missing," I said, and Tony looked at me as if he couldn't care less.

"My feet have never been this tired, even in the army," he said. "Why didn't you warn me not to wear business shoes?"

"I didn't think of it," I said offhandedly. I was more concerned about protecting the kids.

"I'm pooped. It wasn't easy playing father and protector. We must have walked every inch of Central Park. It's beautiful and the sea lions are nice, but I've seen enough."

"Tony! Could you get your mind off your feet? Something's not right. I know it!"

He leaned back on the couch. "Okay, okay, calm down."

He only had to look at me with those big brown eyes and my heart slowed to a normal pace. That sexy look was getting to me. He pounded one of the couch pillows with his fist and curled up in the fetal position. I was losing him to sleep.

I lifted his legs and sat down beside him. His calf muscles were bulging and hard. I massaged them and he moaned.

"Help me," I said. "Think about what we can do."

"Higher," he said, pointing to his thighs. "I think we're doing everything we can."

I crawled out from under his legs and knelt down in front of the couch. Tony stretched out and turned to face me. His pecs called to me. Where were the tit clamps when I needed them? I undid his shirt, button by button, opened it, and then ran my fingers in circles over his chest. His eyes fluttered after a sleepy moan. I cupped his head in my hands and slipped my tongue between his lips. He opened himself to my kiss. Then, he wrapped his arms around my neck and pulled me close.

"We better be careful," I whispered and pointed to my bedroom.

"Uh-huh." His mouth clamped down on mine.

I massaged his cock through his pants. My god, it was big and as hard as an iron bar.

"Careful is right," he said after we released our lip-lock. "Accidents can happen. Are you sure this arrangement with Ophelia is the right thing to do?"

"Yes. More than ever."

I imagined us alone in the apartment while the kids were off playing on the Lower East Side. A far-flung fantasy, but a nice one. My own erection was bursting to break out of my jeans. We kissed and played happily for several minutes until I heard a stirring from the bedroom.

Ruthie appeared in the door, rubbing her eyes with her hands.

"Uncle Des," she said. "A man was standing outside on the sidewalk. I could see his feet."

My heart jumped. The bedroom looked out on the street, as did the kitchen. Both windows were barred and I knew there was no way someone could get in, but a man with a gun could fire through it. Tony and I leaped from the couch and ran to the kitchen window. We looked out, but there was nobody in front of the apartment. Mrs. Lonnigon walked by with a bottle of Irish whiskey in a bag, as she did nearly every day at this time. Her sensible shoes, support hose, and gray coat always gave her away.

"Maybe it was just a neighbor," I said to Tony.

"Maybe." He turned to Ruthie. "How long was he there?"

"I don't know. I woke up 'cause I heard you making noise. He was standing there and then he left."

"What kind of pants was he wearing?" I knew Ruthie had to be looking up through the slats because the blinds were closed in the down position.

"All kinds of different colors—brown and black and orange."

"Camouflage pants," I said. "A bit out of the ordinary for Forty-Seventh Street, but nothing is impossible in New York."

"Come on," Tony said. "Who wears camouflage pants in New York City?"

"Anybody who gets off on army/navy surplus. There must be a dozen stores in Times Square that sell those things. I told you something was wrong."

Tony nodded and then said, "They've got to have better protection."

"Well, you know my plan," I said, and patted him on the back.

We were extra cautious when we took the kids to dinner at Han's. We left the guns at home figuring we didn't need to get involved in a shoot out in Midtown with children in the crossfire. I volunteered to step out first and scour the area. Han's wasn't that far from my apartment, but there were lots of buildings in between. I checked out everything in the immediate area—alleys, the rooftops I could see, anybody who looked as if they were loitering on the street, anyone sitting in cars—nothing seemed out of place. It was an ordinary November day in New York, but the thought of a murderer out to get the kids gave me the creeps. When I was fairly certain everything was okay, I went back for the others. We headed to the restaurant with me in front of Ruthie and John. Tony walked behind.

Norm was going over receipts at the back register when we walked in. His eyes widened and his face broke into a big grin. He dropped the pieces of paper next to the cash register and ran toward me with open arms.

He kept repeating my name and telling me how glad he was to have me back. Now he could get rid of his sister-in-law as dishwasher, he said.

I hugged him. "It's been less than a week, Norm."

"Seems like a hundred years. I told you it wasn't going to be pretty." Norm eyed the kids and Tony.

The front of the restaurant was full of diners, but I didn't want to be there anyway. I directed Tony and the kids to a booth near the back, away from the windows, and introduced them to my boss.

"This is Tony," I said. "And these are the kids, Ruthie and John."

John extended his hand and Norm, with a look of surprise, shook it. "What a little gentleman," my boss said.

"I think he turned out pretty well considering the circumstances," I said.

Norm smiled at Tony and then turned to me and whispered, "My, you've been busy. A husband and *two kids* in less than a week. How did you do it?"

"Tony isn't my husband and the kids aren't ours."

Norm handed me some menus. "Oh, illegitimate."

"Cut the clowning and get us some pot stickers."

"Right away. But when are you coming back to work?"

I handed the menus to Tony and then turned back to Norm. "When do you want me?"

"Tomorrow."

I nodded. "I'll be here."

"Bless you." He winked and tilted his head toward Tony. "What a hot guy. You could do a lot worse. I'd keep him if I were you."

I sometimes wondered if Norm wasn't a tad too gay friendly even though he had a wife and three kids. At any rate, Norm was ecstatic to see us. I could tell by the amount of free food he pushed our way. First, the pot stickers. Wonton soup. Egg-drop soup, egg rolls, shrimp rolls—and those were the starters. Then came the egg foo yung, chow mein, chicken with mixed vegetables, beef, and seafood. In an hour, we were stuffed. The kids had noodles down their fronts and laughed themselves silly trying to use chopsticks. I was shoveling down an order of moo shoo chicken when I noticed the television picture above the cash register.

I poked Tony in the ribs and looked up at the screen. He took the hint. Fortunately, Ruthie and John were facing the street, looking in the opposite direction.

Pictures of Rodney Jessup's funeral flashed across the evening news. Tony and I watched as Carol arrived at the funeral home in a limo. She was wearing a long dark coat that covered her body from her throat to her ankles. A single strand of white pearls lay against her neck. Abby, also attired in black, followed her out of the limo. Both were wearing sunglasses and black hats.

The camera scanned the crowd as the two women worked their way down the carpet toward the door. They looked as if they were attending a Hollywood premiere. Police lined either side of the walkway. The camera rose to an overhead shot and I stopped mid-bite.

A woman wearing a black veil looked from side to side and then up at the camera. I wouldn't have noticed, but she was the only female in the crowd whose face was covered and she seemed more intent on watching what was going on than crying tears for Rodney. Tony nudged me. He had noticed her, too. The newscast repeated the clip of Carol exiting the limo once more and then cut to a long shot of the burial site, far away from the mourners. The telephoto lens picked up the woman with the veil. She was hanging back behind the funeral tent near a line of cedar trees. It was clearly the same person. The newscaster then moved on to a story about Thanksgiving air travel.

"Did you see that?" Tony asked in a hushed voice.

The kids' ears went up after noticing that we were absorbed in something else besides food.

"What's wrong?" John asked.

"Nothing," Tony said. "Do you want dessert? How about fried ice cream and a fortune cookie?"

Ruthie and John smiled like they were going to Disneyland.

I put in the order and then turned to Tony. "I think we have a visual."

"They're working as a pair, aren't they?" Tony asked, knowing the answer to his own question. "That's why Abby thought she saw a woman the night the doll was thrown in the backyard."

"I'd say so."

"We're in double trouble."

I nodded. "After we finish here, we've got to get the kids to Ophelia's as soon as possible. I'd suggest taking them by car rather than by subway."

Tony nodded, but his face drooped, signaling his lackluster enthusiasm.

Something struck me after I saw the woman in the crowd, but I hadn't mentioned it to Tony yet. A call to Carol Kingman Jessup was going to be my second priority of the evening.

But before that thought left my head, I noticed something wrong. Ruthie's eyes bugged out of her head. It was one of those "Oh, shit," moments, but Ruthie wouldn't have articulated it that way, unless she was on her way to appropriating Carol's penchant for profanity.

Before I could ask what was wrong, something zinged over our heads and a red-and-black lacquered lantern crumpled in an explosion of paper and dust.

Glass cracked behind us in a shower of bullets. Then, screams and the sounds of chairs and tables overturning resounded throughout the restaurant.

Tony and I jumped across the booth simultaneously, sending our bodies flying through the sticky remains of rice, chow mein, and chicken with mixed vegetables. I shielded John while Tony took Ruthie. The four of us landed in the rear of the booth. With our backs to the windows, we pushed the kids to the floor.

"Stay put! Don't come out until we say so!" Tony and I huddled in the seat as several more bullets streaked overhead, piercing holes in the back walls.

A deathly pall fell over the room before the slow scrape of chairs and tables entered my ears. A woman cried from the front of the restaurant. A man moaned and then coughed.

Tony and I had formed a spoon in the booth. When I looked up, all I could see was Norm from the chest down. With shaking hands, he was holding a tray of fried ice cream.

Tony and I unraveled from each other. "Stay here with the kids," he said, and brushed past Norm.

The fool was running for the door. Once a cop, always a cop. "Watch yourself," I yelled.

Norm put the tray of ice cream on the table and managed, after a few moments, to get words out of his barely working mouth. "Was this your doing? Was that the guy who gave you the tape?"

I crawled out of the booth and motioned for Ruthie and John

to remain under the table. I ducked my head under it. "Are you both okay?" I asked.

They nodded and scooted back toward the wall. "Was that the man outside your window?" Ruthie asked.

"I think so, sweetie." I turned to Norm. "I tried to warn you that being me wasn't as glamorous as you thought."

"I guess the hell not." I could tell he was in shock. He wasn't even paying attention to the other diners.

"Norm, maybe someone's hurt. Don't you think we should check on your customers?"

He nodded, but I could tell his head wasn't on straight. He was in a place he'd never been before.

I looked back under the table at Ruthie and John. Both were wide-eyed with wonder at what had happened. "Pretend you're bear cubs hiding in a cave from a hunter and the big papa bear will be home soon to save you." They looked at me with horror on their faces. It wasn't the best excuse to keep them under the booth, but it was the only one I could come up with at the moment.

Han's looked a lot worse for wear. The shooter had made a fucking mess—which was putting it politely. The two plate-glass windows looking out on the street were riddled with bullet holes about three quarters of the way up to their tops. One had cracked in half all the way down and was holding together precariously; the other bowed in, as if about to pop from the carnage. Glass was scattered about a third of the way into the restaurant. Two or three other lanterns had also been exterminated.

Diners were dragging themselves off the floor. One woman in a white blouse had blood on her sleeve. A man was holding his hand up to the left side of his face. A trickle of blood ran down his cheek onto his collar. Miraculously, no one was dead or, on the face of it, severely injured.

That was no miracle, however. I surmised that the party pooper who had ruined our nice dinner probably wasn't carrying an M16A2, the assault rifle Tony suspected had killed Rodney. No, this was damage, but only enough to scare the bejeezus out of all of us. Besides, he'd have to have a pretty clever concealment device to cart a military-style weapon through Midtown Manhattan. I couldn't imagine what that would be. Violin cases went out with Prohibition and gangster movies. Maybe a really long quiver? No, that was too crazy. Still, we were in New York.

Norm looked lost tending to the injured diners. I took over for him. Other than elevated heart rates and disbelief, nothing looked serious—only a few minor cuts from flying glass.

I saw Tony flying up the street. Sirens blared behind him. *Oh god*, I thought, *more cops, more questioning.*

He burst through the door and asked Norm to lock it until the police came. Then, he ran to me. "Get the kids and get out of here. Is there a back way out?"

"Gladly," I said and pointed toward the kitchen.

"I'll handle the cops. We don't want Ruthie and John in the papers. I'll tell Norm we need to stick to the story that I was dining alone."

I cocked my head toward the table with the remains of five plates of food. "They'll think you're a big eater."

He shoved me toward the table. "Just get them and get out of here. Everybody else needs to stay. The cops will interview witnesses separately."

Tony didn't need to ask me twice. I coaxed Ruthie and John out from under the booth, grabbed their hands, and headed for the kitchen.

"Bye, Norm," I said. "See you tomorrow."

He looked at me, mouth agape, and shook his head.

I pushed open the kitchen door. No one was inside. Something rustled in the corner, and I saw the two cooks and Norm's sister-in-law huddled between a refrigerator and the wall. I figured they couldn't get into Norm's office, the most logical place to escape the shooter, because it was locked.

Norm's sister-in-law sneered at me. I'm sure she wasn't happy about washing dishes. As soon as Norm filled her in, she'd have another reason to be mad at me.

Triple trouble. When we got back to the apartment, I knew something was wrong. Someone had tried to jimmy the door, but hadn't made it through the double security lock. The scratches and indentations made that clear; it looked to me as if a small crowbar had been used—the kind you could easily hide under a jacket. I didn't have to be Sherlock Holmes to figure out who had tried to get into my apartment. He might have tried before he shot up Han's, or maybe after he left. He probably got interrupted mid-break-in. Who knew? Mrs. Lonnigan might have stood on the sidewalk with her whiskey bottle and stared at him. I pushed Ruthie and John against the door and looked over my shoulder. I fumbled with the key.

Once inside, the kids collapsed on the couch. We were all covered in food, and a bath seemed to be the next order of business.

The blinds were shut so I didn't need to check them. In the living room, I turned on a pole lamp I had scavenged from the street. After the kids were settled, I ran bathwater for Ruthie. She was a trooper and marched straight to the bathroom. I stood outside the door to make sure she'd be okay. She seemed well acquainted with the ways of soap and water.

John sat on the edge of my bed and waited for his turn. I kept the room dark. The only light was from the soft glow of the floor lamp as it spread in a long rectangle across the bed.

"Uncle Des?" John's voice quivered with the question.

"Yes."

"Why is this man trying to kill us?"

His question knocked the wind out of me. I wanted to say

something snarky—make light of the whole mess—but I knew the subject was too serious and the kid deserved an honest answer. I took a deep breath.

"He killed my father, didn't he?" John asked.

I stepped away from the door a minute. I wanted to sit by him and hold him in my arms. "Probably . . . but we don't know that yet." The situation was delicate—I didn't want to frighten him to death. "Your father was a famous man. Sometimes famous people make enemies whether they want to or not. That's what Tony and I are trying to figure out. We're going to bring your father's murderer to justice."

The words drained out of me and my eyes welled up. I thought of Stephen Cross. What justice did he have? The suicide of a crazy man? No. Sometimes life wasn't fair, and justice wasn't always served. Maybe it was time Ruthie and John—at least John so that he could watch over his little sister—knew how difficult catching this killer might be.

As the soft light fell across John's face, I pictured him as a man. One sturdy and strong. I felt he'd be a good man—one who knew right from wrong. One who might marry, have kids, bring them up right, and make them productive members of society. John could make the world a better place, as corny as that platitude might sound. That's what I wanted. That was my goal too after a really shaky start.

I sat beside him. "I want you to be really grown up about this for the next few days. I'm not asking you to take on anything you can't do. Look out for your sister. Always make sure you're both safe. You're going to be staying with a friend of mine—a good friend who will take care of you. But I want you to watch out for yourself and Ruthie."

John nodded.

"We're going to get the guy who's causing all this trouble. There are good guys and bad guys in the world. I don't want you to worry that he's out for you. You can't live your life that way. We'll all be safe. Tony and I will make sure of that." I leaned over and kissed him on the forehead. A lump formed in my throat. It was the first time in my life I had kissed a child.

Ruthie appeared at the door with a towel draped around her like a white evening gown. I dried her off and got her into fresh clothes. John went into the bathroom and closed the door.

Ruthie and I were looking at one of my travel books in the living room when Tony walked in.

He threw his keys on the kitchenette table and plopped down next to us. We didn't speak for a few minutes. Ruthie nodded against my shoulder.

"Well, how did things go with the cops?" I finally asked.

"Just peachy," Tony said.

I snickered. "Hardly think so."

Dripping wet, John stepped into the living room with a towel wrapped around his waist.

"Should I get ready for bed?" he asked.

"No," I said. "We're going for a ride. Put on some clean clothes. Just throw the dirty ones in the corner with Ruthie's. I'll take care of them. Make sure you have everything in your suitcase."

He disappeared into the dark room.

"I can see the Ophelia Cox issue has been decided," Tony said.

"You still have reservations after what happened tonight?"

Tony shook his head. "Can't say that I do."

I put my hand on his arm. "You're sounding awfully Southern. What happened at Han's?"

Tony leaned back against the couch. "I had to be a good ole boy. Again. That's what forced me out of the fraternity in the first place." He stretched out his legs and stared up at the ceiling. "Thankfully, Norm played along. I couldn't have done it without him. I was 'visiting' a friend, happened to be in the restaurant for dinner. Norm told the staff not to mention you and the kids.

I guess the other customers were so shook up, they didn't even notice that you left."

"This was a warning—a show of what he could do," I said.

"Yep. He could have taken everyone out in the first quarter of the restaurant, reloaded, and taken out the rest of us if he wanted to. All he needed to do was step inside the door."

Ruthie pushed away from me and nodded off in the corner of the couch.

"Some kind of high-caliber automatic pistol, I'd say, the way it made mincemeat of those lanterns."

"The cops were taking bullets out of the wall when I left."

"Did anyone see him? Get a description?"

Tony turned toward me. "The woman who got cut got the best look at him. And that wasn't much. I talked to her for a minute before the PD took over. White male. Clean cut. Thirtyish. Semi-handsome. He slipped on a black ski mask when he fired. He walked up to the window—not that anyone would particularly notice him looking at a window menu—slipped the mask on, took his shots, and then got the hell out of Dodge. Hoofed it north and disappeared into the city."

"Someone had to see him on the street."

"When he started firing, people took off or ducked for cover. That's all the cops would tell me."

I sighed. "He knows this city. That's the scary part."

Tony straightened up and smacked his thighs with his palms. "Well, guess we should get the kids to Ophelia's."

"Thought you'd come around."

I told Tony to get the Crown Vic out of the garage and then come back for us. In the meantime, I would try to reach Carol. After Tony left, I checked all the blinds and locks and settled Ruthie and John in front of my old portable radio. They were suddenly kids again. They both complained about not having a television set. I told John that when he was older and earning his own money he could buy any television he wanted. I knew what he was used to watching in Virginia.

I called Ophelia and told her we would be there within the hour. After we hung up, I dialed the motel in Virginia hoping to be connected to Carol. Abby answered.

"How did it go today?" I asked.

"I was nervous as hell, but it was fine. Security was tight. I kept my eyes open."

"Did you see a woman wearing a veil? She stood out in the crowd." I told her about the news report we had seen at Han's.

The line was silent for a moment and then she said, "No." She seemed stunned that Tony and I had noticed anything suspicious. "I'll get the cops on it."

"Listen . . . everything's okay, but something happened tonight at Han's."

Abby's breath caught. "What?"

"Our boy fired into the restaurant. Ruthie and John were there with us, but they weren't hurt. A few of the diners had minor injuries. Don't let Carol find out yet. She'll freak out. You might hear about it on the news. Just gloss over it."

"Okay." Abby sounded unconvinced.

"Can I speak to Carol?"

"Sure. She's in the next room having a drink—of course. But we have adjoining suites so I can keep an eye on her. We'll be in Virginia for a while longer because she has to take care of some estate matters. We'll be in New York the Friday after Thanksgiving. I'm *not* looking forward to the holiday."

Abby put down the phone. It crackled for a minute and then Carol came on the line. She sounded tired, depressed, and about two sheets to the wind—not quite three. We exchanged as many pleasantries as we could before we ran out of polite things to say. She wanted to talk to the kids so I complied, but not before whispering to them that what happened at Han's was our little secret. I monitored the phone call carefully, at the ready to grab the phone out of their hands if I needed to. After they were through telling her about the Chinese food they ate, I took the phone back and asked the question that had been on my mind since I'd seen the funeral footage.

"Do you have any friends?" I asked.

A brutal question, but necessary.

"Of course I have friends," Carol said somewhat indignantly. "I have thousands of friends." She paused and I heard the flare of a match and the sound of cigarette smoke being sucked into the lungs.

It made me want to light up.

"Do you talk to these thousands of friends every day?"

"Of course not. What the hell are you getting at?"

"Who do you talk to every day?"

I had her because her hesitancy to answer vibrated over the line. The details of her personal life were sacrosanct.

"This is important, Carol. The first night we met in Virginia, I asked you if there was anyone who might be intent on destroying your family. When I asked that question, you gave a look like you wanted to answer but couldn't. It was a quick flash and then it was gone. Do you remember?"

She sighed. "I'd had a couple of drinks that day. I'd just looked at my husband's bullet-riddled body. What do you fucking expect?"

It was my turn to sigh. "Think about what you're going to say because Ruthie and John's lives may be in the balance."

Carol sobbed into the phone and then said, "You're trying to destroy me. You and the rest of your queer friends made our lives hell. Can't you leave us alone? Can't you see what you did?"

"I was only trying to get at the truth. Rodney was lying, Carol. He knew Stephen Cross and was afraid to say so because his political career would have been destroyed."

"It was destroyed anyway." Ice tinkled in a glass. "I get nasty when I get drunk. Rodney was the opposite. Liquor made him mellow, smoothed him out after a rough day. He was hard to deal with when he was sober. He was always spouting religion and telling us what to do. I tried to support him, tried to make him see that he was a good person—that he didn't need religion to be a good human being. I was the one who wanted to adopt Ruthie and John because he never wanted . . . . I'm talking too much."

"Please answer the question."

"I talk to Janice Carpenter."

I'd met Janice at the church in New Hampshire. She was Rodney's smart and pretty public relations go-to.

"We talk nearly every day," Carol said. "She was really supportive through this whole ordeal."

"So, Janice knows where you are and what you do."

"Yes. But Janice wouldn't have murdered Rodney. The thought is ridiculous. Besides, she was in Richmond the day he was shot. She adored Rodney and stood by his side when others deserted him. She would never be involved in anything like this."

"Maybe not, but who knows who she talks to."

The ice tinkled again. "She doesn't talk to anyone. Janice and I keep our secrets."

"Thanks for telling me. It gives Tony and me something to go on. The kids are safe and we'll keep them safe. You can count on that." Tony knocked, unlocked the door, and came in. "I've got to take care of Ruthie and John, but let me leave you with one thought, Carol. If God can desert you, so can your friends. Don't talk to Janice for a while. Okay?"

Carol sniffed and then said, "Okay."

It would be hard for her not to talk to her only friend in the world. So much for her thousands of well-wishers. We hung up. It was time to get the kids to their babysitter.

Tony asked me if there was any other exit to my apartment.

I laughed. "I'm lucky to have a front door." He was looking for an escape route with the kids. I told him we could crawl through the kitchen window, but we'd have to saw through the security bars first.

Tony had parked the Crown Vic a few parking spaces away from my apartment. To be safe, we asked the kids to put dark towels over their heads and run to the car. They looked like little licorice sticks running down the street. I went first with their bags. Tony followed Ruthie and John and climbed into the car after them. I hoped we were less of a target at night than during the day. However, a good marksman with a night telescopic sight could still do major damage.

Tony sped off like a New York cabbie and I watched in the rearview mirror. No one was following us. It reminded me of the time I had taken a taxi home from the Roxy dance club at four in the morning. The cab driver hit sixty miles per hour on Tenth Avenue. I went airborne in the backseat at several intersections as we headed uptown. A few pedestrians, flirting with death by jaywalking across a New York City avenue, narrowly escaped with their lives as we whizzed by. No one could have followed me that evening either.

I directed Tony to Ophelia's and we were a bit more relaxed by the time we got to the Lower East Side.

As we pulled into a parking spot about a half a block away from her apartment, I prepared the kids. "Uncle Robert is a little different from what you might be used to."

John looked at me suspiciously and asked, "What do you mean?"

"It'll be fun staying with him," I said.

I held my breath when we rang the Martin/Cox buzzer.

"Come in, darlings," came the breathy reply.

Ophelia's voice seemed cordial and happy, much more like her old self.

When we got to her apartment, the door was open. Tony whistled under his breath.

SHE was back.

The lights were dimmed, the skyline twinkled in the background past the rooftops. Strategically placed candles cast soft shadows about the room. Ophelia, dressed from neck to toe in a long-sleeved, sequined red evening gown, stood in its center. She wore a brunette wig that fell in soft curls across her shoulders. Her lips were painted with ruby-red lipstick and her eyelids were traced with sparkly silver. A large, white, beaded necklace graced her throat. An equally long set of matching earrings completed the look.

"Come in," she said softly.

Ruthie and John stared, but didn't move.

I guided them into the room and said, "Ruthie and John, I'd like you to meet your aunt Ophelia. She's going to be taking care of you for a few days until your mother arrives."

"I thought you said we were meeting Uncle Robert," John said.

Ophelia jangled the bracelet on her wrist. "Uncle Robert and Aunt Ophelia can't be together in the same room. Tonight, you get Ophelia."

"Wow," John said.

Ruthie smiled and held out her hand.

I grabbed Tony's arm and led him to Ophelia. "Tony, I'd like you to meet Ophelia Cox."

"Charmed," Ophelia replied and bowed slightly in her tight gown.

"Likewise, I'm sure," Tony said.

I nudged him. "Didn't I tell you Aunt Ophelia was a knockout?" I was thrilled that Ophelia was feeling well enough emotionally and physically to showcase her old self. She'd always had a thing for glamour and a touch of romance.

Tony nodded. "Yeah, but I don't think you prepared me for the shock—a nice one of course."

"Ophelia has that effect on everyone she meets. She certainly made an impression on me when we met."

We looked at each other for a time with uneasy smiles before Ophelia said to Ruthie and John, "Tonight we're going to play dress up. I've already chosen your outfits."

John pulled his bag to the couch, sat down, and said, "I'm not dressing in girls' clothes."

Ophelia laughed. "Don't be silly. You're going to be a pirate— with a sword and silver earrings and a parrot. All real pirates wear earrings and have a pet parrot."

"What am I going to be?" Ruthie said.

"A princess."

Ruthie clapped her hands. "Where's my dress?"

"Both of them are on the chair," Ophelia said and pointed to her bedroom. "But don't put them on yet. I want to make sure everything's perfect."

Ruthie ran to the room and I heard a squawk.

"You have a live parrot?" I asked.

"No," Ophelia said. "I can't keep animals in the apartment. It's a toy I got years ago at a thrift shop. I do most of my shopping at thrift shops."

John ran to see the bird.

"I named the parrot Sailor. He's a nice bird, but he has a tendency to swear."

Tony looked at Ophelia and then at me.

"I sometimes put words in his mouth," Ophelia said, "but I suppose it's nothing these kids haven't heard."

"They've been pretty sheltered," Tony said.

"Carol's not exactly a saint in the language department," I said. "I'm sure whatever they do here will be an experience they won't forget."

"Probably life altering," Tony said.

I hugged Ophelia. "Everyone should be so lucky as to spend a night playing dress up with Ophelia Cox." I pointed to the couch.

We had some serious matters to discuss before we left. The kids laughed in Ophelia's bedroom.

I began, "I can't thank you enough for taking care of them. Tony or I can be here in the evenings if you have to work."

Ophelia relaxed against the cushions. "The job is important, but not that important. If I have to take a couple of days off, I can. I just can't be out over Thanksgiving weekend. If I am, I'll get fired—and I need the money." She looked down and smoothed her dress with her palms. "I got the info on the pills. It's five hundred dollars for a bottle of ten. It's all black market now. The side effects can be serious, but some men are doing well on them."

I didn't care what the pills cost. "I can get you the money tomorrow. I'll bring a thousand over. Give it a try." All that mattered was that they worked.

Tony looked at me like I was crazy, but he didn't understand yet how far I was willing to go for my friends.

"What do you have in mind for tomorrow?"

"I was thinking of taking them to the zoo and aquarium in Brooklyn. We could all use some fresh air."

"Maybe that's not such a good idea after what happened tonight," I said. I briefly filled in Ophelia on the shooting at Han's, with the mention that their mother shouldn't know the kids were in the restaurant. "I bribed the kids the first night and told them they could go to Central Park with Tony. It was hard enough for him to keep an eye on them the next day. I'm not sure how much this pair knows about our actions. They know where I live. We've tried to be careful, but they might know where you live, too."

Tony nodded. "Isn't there some place around here they could play that's more secure?"

Ophelia laughed. "My apartment is all they'll need for a playground—I've got plenty of trinkets to keep them occupied."

Tony rolled his eyes.

Ophelia glanced at her beautifully polished nails. "And this building has an enclosed courtyard in back. It's large enough to keep two kids happy."

"That would be perfect," I said.

"Believe me," Ophelia said, "I've been keeping my eyes open for years. No one's going to touch those kids."

"We need to be getting home," I said. "Call us if you need to. Tony and I have business to take care of."

Ophelia cocked an eyebrow and said, "I'm sure you do." She looked directly at me, acting as if Tony weren't in the room. "And, by the way, I think he's very handsome. Much better than the riffraff you usually hang out with. I think he just needs to loosen up a little."

Except for the "riffraff" comment, which I assumed was a joke, Ophelia was correct. "He's former army and an ex-cop. A tight-ass. What do you expect?"

Ophelia looked at me and said, "I expect you'll end up in love."

Tony and I managed weak smiles. It was time to say good-bye to the kids and get home.

On the way back to the apartment, I filled Tony in on my telephone call with Carol and her almost daily conversations with Janice Carpenter. Tony had met Janice a few times and thought she was a driven, calculating, professional woman, but not one capable of murder. Having seen it all in my lifetime, I, of course, never put murder past anyone. We also considered the fact neither one of us had seen the name Carpenter on the Ralston's log, although that really didn't mean much.

We parked the car in the garage and walked to the apartment. The temperature had dropped during the evening and the wind blew icily down the side streets. I snuggled next to Tony and he reached for my hand. Tony and I kept our eyes on approaching doorways and rooftops. I felt a little starry-eyed, but still on edge when we got to my door. He stopped me before I could pull out the keys. He glanced at the surrounding buildings, stared at me, and then cupped my face in his hands. Heat roared through my veins.

"Our first real night alone," he said. "At your apartment, in your bed. Should we?" He kissed me.

"Should we what?" I asked, playing dumb.

Tony seemed a bit crestfallen. "Be serious. Have sex."

I thought for a moment, still in the mood to tease him. "I think we should wait. Every time we start, we get interrupted. Making love to you seems to be a dangerous proposition. I don't want to tempt fate."

He kissed me again and I melted into him.

When we finally came up for air, he said, "I was thinking the same thing."

I pushed him away. "What? I was kidding. I'd like to jump your bones on the stoop."

He leaned against the door frame and his eyes twinkled like diamonds in the reflected streetlight. "Cody, I'm not kidding. I really, really, want to, but I don't want our relationship to cloud our judgment. We need to stay sharp—not roll out of bed at ten in the morning after a night of wild, animal sex."

"Sounds great to me," I said seriously.

"Besides, we have a few issues to work out." He inhaled deeply in a dramatic way, waiting for me to beg him to continue.

I took the bait. "Okay. Like what?"

"Oh, like who's the top and who's the bottom?"

I grabbed his jacket and pulled him toward me. "If that's all that's holding you back, I can be versatile."

I kissed him hard and responded in a way that few men had been able to elicit in me. I fused against him; blue waves of electricity flowed from his body into mine. I shivered under my clothes while goose bumps rose on my arms and legs. I was smitten.

He broke away from me long enough to ask, "And what if one of us dies? Have you considered that? We're on dangerous business."

I looked at the Manhattan skyline. For an instant, the world was perfect. A man I was falling head over heels for was in my arms. I felt safe and warm and all those other gooey things one would see in a Hallmark movie. I was pretty sure our hit man wasn't around—at least I hoped so. Nothing spoils a good romance like gunshots.

I ran my hands over his chest and then sagged against the door. "Of course, I've thought about it. I didn't want to bring it up because who *wants* to think about death? I've seen too much of it. I've had my fill."

But, Tony had a point and not an idiotic one. He was different from other men. There was a connection in my soul that was beginning to rise and flower, and I'd never felt anything like it. The feeling wasn't just about sex, and, to be honest, I wasn't sure what to do with these emotions. The men I had loved before Tony had been off limits in one way or another, like Stephen Cross, for example. There was always something standing in the way: alcohol, drugs, sexual addiction, a partner, a marriage. Tony had none of that baggage. An available man for me was as rare as a first edition of Truman Capote. The flush of sexual excitement was a powerful drug, producing a high that had dropkicked many a man and woman to the gutter. Pressing my body against Tony's, feeling his breath on my neck, and kissing his lips were about as good as it could get for me these days. But if I had to step back and think about it, commitment and availability scared the shit out of me. It was a brave new world.

I dug the keys out of my pocket and opened the door. "You're probably right," I said as we stepped inside and switched on the floor lamp. "We've got work to do and sex will get in the way." I had cooled off.

Tony put his hands on my shoulders. "Hey, look, I don't mean never. I just meant maybe we should slow down until we get through this."

"You're right. Want to sleep on the couch?"

Tony laughed. "I was in the army. I know how to control my urges."

In a way, I was sorry he had that control because his constancy assured me of another long night. It would be a night with no sex and little rest because I'd keep myself awake thinking about the naked man sleeping next to me, while also wondering whether there was a killer lurking outside my apartment.

New York City never sleeps, but there is a time of night, between the hours of four and six a.m., when the city slows down. Cabs aren't as frequent, traffic is rarely hung up. A ride of ten minutes from the Village to Midtown isn't unheard of.

During those hours, when people drag themselves from the bars or leave their secret lover to sneak home before dawn, only the hardiest New Yorkers are out. Or the craziest.

That's why after getting into bed well after eleven p.m., the lightbulb suddenly blazed on in my head. If Ruthie could see the man upward through the slats during the daytime, then the man would be able to see us when they were pointed downward at night if there was any kind of light in the apartment. I had left the floor lamp on.

"We have to move to the living room," I said. "And turn off all the lights." I could have turned the slats into the up position, but either way I felt better knowing we were out of range of our trigger-happy friend. He could easily take a few pot shots through the bedroom window while we were sleeping.

Tony was already half asleep when I made the decision to move.

"Why?" he asked, stretching out in bed.

I explained my reasoning. Even with all the lights out, there would still be enough light in the apartment from the city's ambient brightness to make our way around the room.

I turned off the lamp. Tony took the couch. I took the floor, making a bed of pillows and blankets. It wasn't as comfortable as my own mattress, but I really didn't feel like dragging it into the living room. Tony and I "touched" good night, and soon he was snoring softly on the couch.

At times like these, vestiges of my former life crept in. I learned early on in my hustling career to sleep with one eye open. The technique had served me well; particularly when I was bedded down on the street overnight—not an uncommon occurrence. It had saved me from pickpockets, downright thieves and, in a few instances, from being murdered in my sleep.

So, at about four thirty a.m., it came as no surprise when a shadow blocked the light in front of the barred kitchen window, which looked out onto the street. It lingered there a fraction of a second too long—at that hour, most people walked swiftly by or stumbled down the street, mirroring their capacity for liquor.

I pulled down the blankets and scooted off the pillows. Tony was on his back on the couch, one arm dangling off it. I was naked and the air felt frosty, but none of that mattered. The shadow disappeared to the right as I headed toward my door. Light from the street came back to the window full force.

I moved swiftly through the room, intent on not making a sound. I got to the sink and shifted my body toward the east side of the window. He would have a hard time shooting me through the glass at that angle. I doubted he could even see me in the darkness.

Something soft thumped against the door. I lifted a slat on the blind and saw a dark figure heading west. No one else was around. The memory of what had happened in Rodney's backyard in Virginia came roaring back.

I left the window and crept over to Tony. I nudged him awake.

Instinctively, he jumped up, about to bark questions at me. I put my hand over his mouth.

"Someone left us a present on the stoop," I said. "Not sure what it is, but I'm getting my Desert Eagle."

Tony shook off sleep and got up from the couch. He was naked, too, and the sight was enough to make me want to forget about Rodney Jessup, Carol, the kids, and the killer. I was on the verge of calling the Pope to nominate me for sainthood when, once again, cold, hard reasoning got in the way.

I sneaked back to my bedroom, grabbed my keys, and retrieved the gun from under the bed. I hadn't worried about Ruthie and John taking naps with the weapon under the bed because they were always unloaded and the shells were hard to reach on the top shelf of my closet.

I loaded the Eagle and moved silently back to the living room.

"I'm going to turn on the light over the door, open it, and stand back," I whispered to Tony. I handed him a pillow. "Throw it across the door to the wall when I signal. If he's outside he may take a shot at it."

Tony nodded and moved toward the sink where he could duck below the window and throw the pillow past the door.

I flipped on the outside light half expecting the door to explode in a flurry of bullets, but nothing happened. I unlocked the locks, flung the door open, and crouched behind it. The cold air rushed in. I lifted my arm in a hatchet throw, pointing to the wall.

The pillow flew past me and landed in a soft crush on the other side of the door.

No gunfire.

I peered around the door from its bottom. No one was in sight. The street, at least in front of my apartment, was empty. I stood up, raced to the stoop, grabbed the paper bag that had been thrown there, raced back inside, and closed the door.

Bombs didn't seem to be this killer's MO, so I wasn't too

worried about the bag exploding in my hands. Presumably, he didn't know if Ruthie and John were inside, so he wouldn't risk planting a bomb. What good would it do to blow them up if he wanted them alive?

"Grab the flashlight," I said. "It's under the sink."

"Do I have to?"

"Don't be a smartass. The cockroaches will leave you alone."

I could have sworn that I saw him shiver when he opened the cabinet doors. He pulled out the black flashlight and switched it on.

I motioned to him. "Come on. You first?"

"No way," he said.

Tony pointed the flashlight at the bag, while I pulled off the rubber band that formed a ring at its top. The bag popped open.

"Shine it inside," I instructed.

Two beady little eyes peered up at me. I squealed and dropped the bag.

Tony jumped back and the beam flashed around the room. "What is it?"

"A rat." I brushed my hands on my thighs. "I think it's dead."

"Oh, is that all," Tony said and approached the bag. He kicked it and nothing moved. "Rats I can handle. Cockroaches and spiders? No. Keep the light on it."

He bent down and looked into the bag. His naked back extending down to the curve of his buttocks distracted me for a moment—only a moment. Tony stuck his hand into the bag and I gagged.

"Jesus," I said. "Ugh. That's gross. Be sure to wash your hands."

"Oh, grow up. There's a message inside. Looks like the little fellow's throat was slit and the blood drained out. Not much in the bag."

"I'm sorry. I'm not feeling any sympathy. I do *not* like rats. Get rid of as many as you want. Rats are not an endangered species, especially in New York."

Tony pulled a piece of notepaper out of the bag. It looked suspiciously like the one I'd found tacked to the tree on the hillside near Rodney's home. He shined the flashlight on the paper, then handed it and the light to me.

Don't be a rat. Rats who don't obey end up dead.

"Charming," I said. "Keep the note and let me get rid of that thing." I opened the door and hurled the bag near the sidewalk. "I'll deal with that in the morning."

Tony was already at the sink washing his hands. I followed his lead and put the flashlight under the sink.

He yawned and stretched his arms over his head. "Can we get back to bed now? Maybe we can catch a few winks before sunrise."

We crawled back into our respective beds. Soon Tony was snoring. Again.

I kept seeing the image of the rat staring up at me from inside the bag. My arms broke out in an itch. As far as I was concerned, the sun couldn't rise fast enough.

CHAPTER TEN

THE NEXT MORNING, I ASKED TONY TO CALL ONE OF the cops he was semi-friendly with in Buena Vista to get Janice Carpenter's phone number. I didn't want to bother Carol. She wouldn't have been happy anyway if she knew I was planning to call her friend to get Janice Carpenter's phone number because it was unlisted.

Tony's call was returned within an hour, as we were finishing breakfast. He scribbled the number on a piece of paper and handed it to me. It was a listing in Richmond.

While Tony showered, I called Janice Carpenter.

"This is Cody Harper," I began when she picked up. "I don't know if you remember me."

The silence on the other end was as solid as concrete. For a moment, I thought the line had gone dead.

"I have nothing to say to you," she finally said, her tone seething with icy hatred.

The receiver clicked with a bang in my ear. No one could misread her feelings about me. I pondered my next move and felt extremely inadequate. When Tony stepped out of the shower, he read the discouragement on my face.

"No go?" he asked, and forced a smile. He wrapped his towel around his waist and sat on the couch.

I looked at the hunk sitting across from me and wondered why the hell I was involved in this mess in the first place. It was easy to blame Rodney, the money, Ophelia, then blame Tony, Carol, and the kids—everyone except myself. Maybe it was time to get this whole bodyguard, save-the-world routine out of my system. Settling down with Tony would make life a hell of a lot easier.

"No go," I said. I tapped my fingers against my kitchenette table. "Janice Carpenter won't speak to me. Maybe you could try to get something out of her." I sighed. "This is driving me crazy. Waiting for this guy to strike is worse than knowing something's going to happen, like when Chris Spinetti and I met in the Déjà Vu. I knew the lid was going to blow then. But now, it's sit and wait. They're out to get the kids and it's making me nuts."

"Patience in all things. They'll play their hand sooner or later."

I settled on the couch. "You know, I guess I could learn a thing or two from you. Be more Zen about this whole thing. We're carrying on, as the English would say."

Tony leaned over and kissed me. The towel slipped off his leg, giving me an enticing view.

I forced my hands behind my back to keep them off him. "You better get dressed, before I go nuts for you. I need to do a few things before I get ready for work. I should call Norm and see if the restaurant is open."

"He was calling window suppliers when I left. He told me he'd be open today come hell or high water. I'll call the cop back and see what kind of background info he can get on Janice Carpenter."

We shook ourselves free of each other and geared up for business. I remembered I had to go to the bank to get a thousand dollars for Ophelia's pills.

* * *

Han's was back to normal the day after the shooting. I kept to my dishwashing job, out of sight, which brought everyone some peace of mind.

Still, Tony and I looked over our shoulders for the next couple of days. I delivered the money to Ophelia, who seemed happier than ever; she was having a ball with Ruthie and John and they seemed to be enjoying themselves as well. A few of the neighbors dropped by, some of whom had small children of their own. They played games inside the apartment. Tony babysat when Ophelia returned to work a couple of nights at Club Leo and I had to work at Han's. He stayed the night with the kids and took care of them in the morning while Ophelia slept. As much as we hoped the killer didn't know about Ophelia and the kids, we couldn't be sure. We were as cautious as we could be, using different modes of transportation to cover our trails and traveling late at night because it was easier to spot someone who might be on our tail. Carol and Abby were delayed a few days in Virginia taking care of the family's business interests.

Paranoia is never a good feeling. I figured all hell was going to break loose when we least expected it.

One morning a package arrived by mail from the Buena Vista Police Department with photocopies of clippings about Janice Carpenter. One from 1994 held our interest. It was a small daily listing no more than two thumbs deep from the Richmond newspaper. We both stared at it as it sat on my small coffee table.

Divorce granted: Stanley Adam Bozelle from Janice Carpenter Bozelle, May 24th, 1994, Hon Judge Asher, Henrico County, presiding. Irreconcilable differences, emotional cruelty. Maiden name, Janice Carpenter, restored.

"He filed? Emotional cruelty from Janice Carpenter?" Tony asked, amazed.

"You've never met her," I said. "She's one hard-baked cookie."

A 1990 clipping caught our eye as well. It was the original marriage announcement of Janice to Stanley Bozelle. *The groom is a graduate of the Officer's Candidate School and served in the US Marines from 1980 to 1986.*

Tony whistled. "Where's the shooting range log?"

"Under the bed, I think." I hadn't looked at it since our first night in New York.

Tony ran to the bedroom and soon reappeared with the log in hand. We both scanned the pages, and it didn't take us long to find what we were looking for, the name, *S. Bozelle,* in blue ink. He had signed in at Ralston's the day before Rodney was murdered.

"Our first real lead," I said.

"But why this guy?" Tony asked, thinking out loud.

"That's for us to find out. But if he's an ex-marine, we need to be damn careful. He's probably a crack shot."

"You can bet on that. I can't imagine anything more dangerous than a crazy jarhead with an assault rifle."

Ideas were beginning to form in my head about our Mr. Bozelle and a lot of them circulated around a sum of half-a-million dollars. What if Rodney Jessup had paid a marine sharpshooter to knock off Stephen Cross, but a small-time right-winger had beaten him to the punch? What if Janice Carpenter was involved in this whole scheme?

I picked up the phone and dialed information for the Richmond area. Tony watched with interest. I wanted a cigarette bad, but since we had been in New York, Tony had forced me to sit on the sink and blow the smoke out through the kitchen window. I made like a chimney while sitting on cold, hard porcelain. I ordered him not to have more than a single glass of wine or beer a night because I didn't want him to reek of alcohol. This was what our blissful domestic life had already come to—a series of compromises.

The phone rang and a woman picked up. I raised the register of my voice and attempted an imitation. "Hello. This is Janice Carpenter. Could I please speak to Stanley?"

The woman on the other end sounded as angry as Janice. "Who is this?"

I repeated Janice's name.

"You're fucking crazy," the woman said. "You're not Janice Carpenter and even if you were, I wouldn't let you speak to *Stanley*. You've never called him 'Stanley' in your life! Get off the phone asshole." She hung up with a loud click.

"Strike two, of sorts." I turned to Tony. "I've managed to piss off two women in a few days. My luck has never been great with the opposite sex."

"Thank god for that."

I walked to the kitchen. I had opened the blinds to let in some light. I looked out through the security bars to the sidewalk. Every few seconds a new pair of feet would walk by. "Now that we know who we're dealing with, I don't think we need to wait any longer."

Tony followed and looked at me with a stare that said, "Are you crazy?" Still, he was so cute I was more than willing to forgive his skepticism.

"Instead of waiting for them to strike," I said, "let's set a trap and see who gets caught."

"Dangerous."

"Yes, but better than being sitting ducks."

Tony reluctantly agreed. We sat together drinking coffee and drew up our plan. It involved the Macy's Thanksgiving Day Parade. But before the holiday arrived, I decided to make a quick trip to Richmond.

"Are you crazy?" Tony stared at me. His fists were clenched and his arms stiff at his side. "You've done some pretty dumb things in your life. I thought you'd gotten smarter hanging around me."

"Come on," I replied. "You've been a cop—you're an investigator. Don't you have the least bit of curiosity about Mrs. Bozelle? At least I can get a look at her. Maybe ask her a few questions."

Tony looked as if I had gut punched him. "Right! You're going to show up at her door like you're coming over for a cup of sugar? You could get yourself killed."

I nodded.

"I can't believe it," Tony sputtered. "What's next? Maybe drag or maybe break into the house, whatever insane tactic you can think of? And, besides, what about the kids?"

"Carol and Abby won't be here until after Thanksgiving. You can help Ophelia with Ruthie and John. What else have you got to do until Bozelle makes his move—except be careful?"

Tony's jaw slackened. He looked dumfounded.

"I can't do drag anyway. Don't have the time or the room to pack a lot of luggage."

"You're a hardheaded donkey, Cody." Tony huffed and sat on the couch. "When are you leaving?"

"Tonight. I've already made the round-trip reservation. I'll be back late tomorrow afternoon. You won't even have time to miss me."

"When did you do this?" Tony crossed his arms. "Don't let me sway you, but I want you to know you're fucking nuts."

"When you were in the shower." I scrunched up beside him and gave him a peck on the cheek. "I called Norm and told him I wouldn't be in for a couple of days. I think he was relieved. I'll be back in time for Thanksgiving, and, by the way, I love you too, darling."

Tony grunted and got up from the couch. "I'm going out for lunch. This apartment is getting awfully close."

He needed to blow off steam so I let him go. I had packing to do.

* * *

Unfortunately, there was no limo waiting for me like the last time I made the trip to Virginia. I locked the apartment, scanned the street quickly, and hailed a taxi at the corner. Tony had already left for Ophelia's without so much as a kiss, though he did wish me a frosty "Good-bye."

The taxi driver was no slouch—a heavy-bearded, working-class, white guy with a hint of body odor, who wove through traffic, giving other drivers the finger or a blast from the horn. He had the heater on hurricane force with the window down. His checkered shirt opened over his chest revealing a thick mat of black fur—he was a type who had high appeal for a certain subset of gay man.

He had me at LaGuardia in twenty minutes. I gave him a decent tip before he blasted off with another fare.

I had booked the last flight of the day to Richmond. This trip, unlike last time, I had no trepidation about getting on the jet. In fact, I was excited about seeing New York at night from a mile high. I pushed my backpack into the overhead bin and settled into my seat. I carried only the essentials: toiletries, a change of clothes, a notebook, and pen. This was definitely a jacket, black jeans, and lumberjack shirt kind of trip—nothing fancy or attention getting.

The jet pulled back from the walkway. Soon we were in the air, the city dropping away like some Disneyland ride with a view through pressurized glass. Tiny dots of light swarmed across roads and highways. Cars clustered in shopping mall parking lots. The Manhattan skyline filled my window until it dropped sharply away into the inky darkness of the Atlantic. After we flew over suburban Jersey, the view got less interesting. Small towns and cities lay in glittering patches below. I took a quick nap and before I knew it we were on approach to Richmond.

After we landed, I rented a car and drove to an inexpensive

motel near the intersection of I-64 and I-295. The desk clerk gave me a map of the city and wished me happy touring. I told him I'd only be there for the night.

In my humble room, I found a phone book and the address for Stanley Bozelle. The address corresponded to a neighborhood called Davee Gardens. I showered, turned off the light, and slept soundly despite the buzz of nearby interstate traffic.

In the morning, I grabbed some juice and cereal at the motel breakfast bar before checking out. The day was bright with some wispy overhead clouds. I'd forgotten to bring my sunglasses. I put my bag in the trunk, checked the map, plotted my route, and drove off. I had no idea what I was headed for.

It didn't take long for me to get to Davee Gardens. The neighborhood was southwest of the motel. The drive only took me about a half hour because rush hour was mainly over. The homes were modest, and the area was pleasant enough with lots of tall oaks still holding on to their brown fall leaves.

I found the address and drove past a small, white clapboard house with a strange pitched-roof room that stuck out like a castle turret. A well-worn ten-year-old Ford was parked in the driveway. The white car had turned a suitable shade of dirty from years of use.

I parked about a block away and sat for about fifteen minutes contemplating my next move. In some ways Tony had been right, I was crazy and I wasn't sure what I was looking for. I wondered if I could get inside the heads of the people who were possibly involved in murdering Rodney Jessup. Maybe looking at the house would spark a clue. Perhaps I could even spot the woman involved, my assumption being that the man was still in New York looking for the kids.

I locked the car and walked down the street feeling strange. I had dressed to look "normal," but what was normal here? I was the proverbial fish out of water. I stood out even in my jeans and shirt, most of all because *no one* was around. The boots clicked on the jumbled concrete walk; leaves crunched under my tread. If there were dogs in the neighborhood they were indoors, cuddled up for a morning nap. No kids played in the yard—it was a school day. The overwhelming quiet gave me the creeps. I felt like Jodie Foster in *The Silence of the Lambs,* walking up to Jame Gumb's house.

This house had a spooky feel to it also. It looked chopped up, somehow disfigured, and unpleasant. The blinds were drawn on the three windows facing the street. The pitched-roof room looked forbidding, coming out as it did from the rest of the structure. A set of ragged wooden steps led up to the entrance. The door was narrow with a tiny rectangular window set above eye level so no one on the outside would be able to look in. Anyone inside would have to stretch or stand on a step stool to look out onto the porch.

A chain-link fence surrounded the yard, but not the driveway. Did the Bozelles have a dog?

I was about a half block away, still taking all this in, when the front door opened. A woman, wearing jeans and a jacket, walked out, suitcase in hand. She was concerned with getting the door locked and didn't notice me. I tried to picture her in black, with a veil, like the woman we'd spotted in the news at Rodney's funeral. She was about the same height, the same body type, but the news clips weren't enough to go on. The camera angle, the crowd, the brief glimpses made it hard to tell if this was the same woman.

She was somewhat pretty, but in a hard way, as if life had been tough. Her hair was shoulder length, brown, and a bit bedraggled; her facial lines were creased and stern. I immediately sensed what her life was like: getting by, money hard to come by, always some bump on the road of life keeping her off balance.

I crossed the street and kept walking toward the house, preferring not to duck behind a tree. She wouldn't have any idea who

I was. On the other hand, I did look out of place at ten in the morning walking alone on the street. I kept my eyes focused straight ahead, hoping to appear like a casual walker, but kept my left eye peripherally engaged on her.

She grabbed her suitcase, walked down the steps into the yard, and through the gate that led to the sidewalk. She glanced my way, but only for a second—nothing out of the ordinary. In less than a minute, her car's trunk had been opened, the case placed inside, and the driveway vacated. The car sped down the street in the direction from which I had come, maybe on its way to the interstate.

I was alone again on the walk. I turned and retraced my steps back to the house. Tony's little angel with white wings stood on my shoulder warning me not to act on the thought that was spinning through my head. My little devil was prodding me on. *Go ahead, break into the house. Don't you want to see what's inside? Maybe there's someone there, but you won't find out until you knock on the door.*

The devil won. I knew he would.

I summed up the situation. The street was dead. There was no time like the present—although I hoped the woman hadn't gone for a spin around the block.

I crossed the street, opened the gate, and walked up the steps. The lawn was in that strange stage between fall and winter, where life had not totally surrendered to death. Some plants had survived the cold weather. A few green sprigs sprouted between the fallen oak leaves and clumps of dead grass. There was no sign of toys or dog droppings. I knew I was standing in front of the Bozelle residence. Stanley was in New York and she was on her way to god knows where, but if I had to guess I'd have said to join him.

What if the neighbors happened to be looking? What would I tell them if they asked? I didn't exactly look official. Phone company? Lineman? Nope. A private investigator with no ID? Probably wouldn't fly.

I knocked and, of course, no one answered. No barking either. A small white mailbox was affixed to the wall on the right of the door, but there was no name on it. I lifted its lid. No mail inside.

I walked around the side of the house, still in the fenced-in yard. A small wooden deck protruded from the back. The deck was accessible from the inside through a set of French doors. I didn't have tools on me, not even a credit card, but I did have a plastic strip in my wallet that I used for such occasions when they came up. Most of the time it lay unused in my back pocket. Frankly, it had been years since I had broken into a house.

I hopped on the deck and looked through the doors. A set of grimy curtains were drawn across them, but there was a narrow gap in the middle, enough for me to see the immediate layout of the house. The kitchen was to the left. Straight ahead, to the center of the house, was the main door, and off to its right was the strange room that jutted out into the yard.

The property was pretty well concealed by brush and mature trees. The Bozelles valued their privacy.

I took out the strip and inserted it into the lock. Luckily, there was no deadbolt on the door. That wouldn't have stopped me, but it did make my job easier. The plastic, stiff but not brittle, fought a battle against the latch three times before the lock yielded.

I pulled the handle and stepped inside. No alarm. I looked around quickly. As far as I could tell there were no surveillance cameras.

The kitchen smelled like bacon and fried eggs. Grease congealed in a pan on a still warm stove. Either the woman was in a hurry or she was a horrible housekeeper.

But there was another distinctive smell that I detected in the air, one that couldn't be mistaken for anything else. The pleasant, metallic smell of gun oil permeated the house. Had the woman been cleaning weapons before she left? What was in that brown leather suitcase? Now I was convinced she was on her way to New York. If my flight was on time, I'd arrive in the city several hours before she got there. I made a mental note to call Tony from the airport.

Everything in the house was cheap, bordering on tawdry—not that I was in any position to talk, considering the state of my apartment. I hadn't really moved up yet to Goodwill chic. Most of the stuff I owned, I had found on the street. Stanley's house had a "lived in" look, devoid of charm. A worn Formica table and two chairs sat in a kitchen corner. The three rooms in the front were bathed in a murky gray light despite the crisp November sun. One of those rooms was a bedroom brimming with disarray. The bureau drawers were open, clothes had been tossed on the floor, and the bed was a tangle of sheets and blankets.

The living room sat in the center of the house. A portable television on a cheap metal stand was pushed in front of the window. A couple of empty beer cans sat on a wobbly coffee table, otherwise populated by hunting and fishing magazines. I looked at the address tape on one of them. Stanley Bozelle—at this address. Another periodical caught my eye. It offered luxury yachts for sale. Clearly, Stanley had big dreams.

For some reason, I dreaded going into the weirdly shaped room that looked as if it had been added as an afterthought. It reminded me of a castle turret without the stairwell. Just looking at it from ten feet away gave me the willies. Equally dark, it sat there like a monstrous maw waiting to swallow me. In fact, I knew that was a good sign, possibly emanating from those gifts of prophecy the Bay Village fortune-teller in Boston had revealed in her reading. Whatever I needed to know was in that room.

I stepped inside. A secondhand desk sat against the north wall, far enough away from the window to be unobtrusive, but close enough to get light if the shades were opened. I switched on the plastic desk lamp sitting on top of it. A circular beam shone down upon the battered wood. A stack of business cards sat in a metal holder. I picked them up and thumbed through them. Nothing struck me except a particular card—from Ralston's, the shooting range. More proof at least one of them had been there. The name of the Range Master was scrawled on the back.

I rummaged through the desk, pulling out papers and replacing them in correct order as best I could. Near the bottom of the pile I found a crude pencil drawing that looked like a fourth grader's bizarre art assignment. On the top half of the picture, a stick figure in camouflage stood in front of a tree line of roughly sketched pines. On the bottom, two stick children kneeled behind a bigger figure holding a gun. It was the perfect recreation of the scene in Rodney Jessup's backyard the night Carol and the kids had returned after their cruise. The larger figure was Abby protecting the smaller stick figures, Ruthie and John, from the camouflage-clad stick figure who threw the bag into the yard. Abby had sensed that the perpetrator was a woman. Perhaps the woman had drawn this for Bozelle. I folded the paper and put it in my jacket pocket. More criminal offenses—but I didn't care.

Something at the back of the room caught my eye, hidden in the gray light. The room was big, higher and wider than the others in the house. The rear wall consisted of two large paneled doors that stretched from floor to ceiling. The two handles, one on each door, were secured with an inexpensive chain and lock that bound the panels together. If there was any play at all in the doors I knew I could get them open. I grasped the handles and pulled. The doors pulled open with enough room to get my fingers inside with two inches to spare. I already had "breaking and entering" and "tampering with evidence" on my rap sheet, why not add "destruction of property" to the list?

I forced my hands into the space above the lock and pulled. After several attempts to open the door, I finally planted one foot against the bottom of the panel and pulled with all my might. The handle popped off with a crack.

The cabinet held an arsenal of weapons. I counted at least twenty high-powered hunting and assault rifles, the makes and models so diverse it was impossible to hold them all in my head. There were also interesting additions to the cache: swords, deadly walking sticks, handcuffs, ninja stars, silencers, camouflage, concealment clothing, and masks.

I pulled a chair over to get to the top of the cabinet. Two shelves, high up, added to my amazement. The Bozelles, if anything, were ready for the apocalypse. Raw gunpowder, shells, a bullet maker, supplies, and gloves were lovingly placed on them. Unlike the house, everything in the cabinet was in perfect, pristine, orderly condition. It reminded me of people who could spend three thousand dollars on fireworks for the Fourth of July, but couldn't afford to paint their house.

A small stash of cash—about a thousand dollars—caught my attention also. I left it alone. I didn't need to add grand larceny to my charges.

I'd seen all I needed to see. These people were armed and dangerous. I was now convinced that Stanley Bozelle was the man who had murdered Rodney Jessup. The remaining question was: What was his motive?

I searched the desk one more time and found a couple of things I'd overlooked. One was a photograph cut from a magazine, or a religious tract, that was stuck in the corner of the drawer. It was a picture of an aborted bloody fetus. I'd seen blood and guts before, but the image turned my stomach. It left me feeling unsettled, but also thinking about why Stanley Bozelle would be out to get Rodney Jessup. Jessup was no fan of abortion, so I doubted his murder was politically motivated. More likely it was personal. I pocketed that picture as well.

The other unusual item was a small silver box with switches

that was concealed behind a standard desk telephone. A connector cord stretched between the phone, a tape message machine, and the box. I wasn't sure what the box was for, but it looked like a sophisticated setup—one you wouldn't find in every Davee Gardens home.

I returned everything to its original place, including putting the damaged handle back on the cabinet doors, and turned off the lamp. The Bozelles were smart enough that it would take them about two seconds to discover that someone had broken into the house. I was glad I would be far away by the time that happened.

I closed the French doors, walked through the yard, and went out the gate to the sidewalk. A man walking a chocolate lab lifted his hand in greeting as he passed by. The dog gave me a couple of sniffs as he lumbered on. His brain was probably fixated on the scent of bacon and fried eggs, not the gun oil.

I walked to the car and sat for a time before starting back to the airport. I had plenty of time to grab lunch before my flight. I wondered if Tony would still be mad about this trip when he found out what I had discovered—or how I discovered it.

At any rate, he needed to know what we were dealing with.

CHAPTER ELEVEN

THE COLD WAR BETWEEN TONY AND ME HAD
thawed a bit by the time I walked in the door. He was sitting on
the couch, but his face was grim, his lips narrowed with tension.

"How was your flight?" he asked.

I took his question as a peace offering.

"Fine." I tossed my bag on the bed and returned to the couch.

"Can we talk now—without anger and recrimination?" I
asked.

I got a half smile from him. "You and your fifty-cent words. I
didn't plan on having a dictionary for a boyfriend."

A boyfriend? Tony had never been generous with his terms of
endearment, but I liked the feeling of being his boyfriend. The
words felt safe and warm. I sat close to him, reached over, and
stroked his hair. The silky strands felt good between my fingers.
Sometimes I got the feeling with Tony that everything in the
world was going to be all right. That song from *Sweeney Todd*
about being safe from harm popped into my head.

"So what did you find out, Mr. Investigator?" Tony asked.
"And how many laws did you break?"

I had told him when I called from the airport that I couldn't talk in public, but I had important information to share.

"About three, by my count." I pulled the crude sketch and the photo from my jacket pocket and handed them to him.

Tony whistled when he saw the drawing. "Holy crap. That's Abby and the kids in Jessup's backyard."

"You've got a second career as an art critic." I snuggled against him.

He looked at the photo and scrunched up his mouth. "What's this about? Pretty disgusting."

"I have no idea, but I'm sure it ties in somehow. We'll find out as soon as he plays his hand." I weaved the fingers of my right hand through his left. "The jackpot of the whole visit was the armory I found in the house. Enough weaponry to start a small war with a Central American country. If I had to guess, I'd say he's the one who killed Jessup. And she's probably just as dangerous as he is."

I described my visit to the house and all the naughty things I had done. Tony shook his head in amazement. "You go where cops fear to tread," he said.

"That's one of the reasons I'm not a cop. To hell with those bureaucratic channels. If no one gets hurt and I save a few lives, all the better." I regretted my last words immediately because my friend Stephen Cross trotted into my head. I hadn't saved him, try as I might. The day I found him in the snow in New Hampshire would be forever etched into my mind. I thought of him every day. A word, a reflection, a piece of clothing could trigger a memory. I tried to forget, but forgetting was one of the most difficult tasks I'd ever had to take on. I could see him in my head as if he were standing in front of me. That clarity provided little comfort. The heartache of losing him was lessening, but the pain still bubbled to the surface now and then.

"Speaking of," I said, hoping to shake the memory. "How are the kids?"

Tony relaxed a bit against me. "They're well and happy. I have to admit that sending them to Ophelia was the best thing to do. I can't imagine them here. When he's not working, he entertains them constantly. Which reminds me . . . "

"What?"

"I have to get over to the apartment. He's working tonight and tomorrow, Thanksgiving night."

Tony stood up and stretched. "He's planning something— something big. It's driving me nuts."

"We're sticking with our plan for tomorrow?"

"Yep," Tony said. "I don't think we have a choice. She'll be in the city by then."

"Probably arriving in about three hours," I added.

Tony showered and headed off to Ophelia's. I took a shower too and thought about dropping in at Han's. Maybe they needed an extra dishwasher for the night. I talked myself out of that. I stretched out on the couch and thought about all the nasty ways Stanley Bozelle could make life difficult for Ruthie and John. My thoughts weren't pleasant.

I had a hunch and I acted on it. I called Janice Carpenter. As on my previous attempt, she was in no mood to talk. However, I told her that the kids and I would be attending the parade and would be standing in Times Square very near the TKTS booth.

"Look for us on TV," I said with a hint of sarcasm.

I barely got the words out of my mouth before she hung up. It was enough time to get the message across and that was what I intended.

I called Ophelia and caught her before she left for Club Leo. I told her that if she was planning to take Ruthie and John to see the parade to make sure she was nowhere near Times Square. In fact, I suggested she camp out by Macy's front door under the glare of national television coverage and in the company of a swarm of New York's finest.

"Whatever you do," I said, "make the kids blend into the crowd."

I could foresee Ophelia's Thanksgiving Day joke: John in a dress and Ruthie in a tuxedo. She would rationalize her behavior as a festive kick-off to the holiday season. Or she might put them in turkey costumes. Whatever they were, I asked her to discuss her plans with Tony.

Thanksgiving Day dawned with broken clouds and moderate temperatures. Winds were light also; always a big factor in handling the large balloons that floated down Broadway to Herald Square annually on this day. As it turned out, this year was the seventieth anniversary of the parade and a large, boisterous crowd was expected. That made it all the better for Tony and me.

First, I dug two large duffle bags out of my closet and stuffed them with pillows. Then, we dressed them in old clothes, from top to bottom, from hats down to the shoes. We attached soft tubing that Tony had purchased—legs and arms—with twine and safety pins. Up close, no one would mistake the bags for kids, but from a hundred yards away and across a crowded street, the artifice might hold up. As Ophelia had taught me, life, with a change of clothes, hairstyle, and makeup, could alter the individual. In that respect, all life was an illusion.

The weather was brisk, so the clothing we chose was appropriate. We would carry our little bundles of joy under our arms until we got to Times Square. We might get a few strange looks, but this was New York—what the hell? Who would care? If we even got a second glance, people would think we were just a couple of wacko New Yorkers getting into the holiday spirit. We both considered taking our guns, but reassessed. We weren't looking for a gunfight on a crowded street filled mostly with kids and parents.

As we carried our "children" to our appointed space about an hour before the parade began, we discussed what we thought might happen.

"He's not out to kill them," I said. "He's after kidnapping money. We need to flush him out. He knows where I live. If I were in his head, I'd wonder if we might take the kids to the parade. It would be hard to deny Ruthie and John that pleasure."

"I still don't understand why he killed Rodney," Tony said. "Why not go after the kids in the first place?"

I had no answer.

We passed Eighth Avenue, heading west on Forty-Fifth Street. A stream of people poured down the sidewalks toward Times Square.

I hefted my child over my shoulder. The shoes flopped against my back. Tony's question roared into my head. "Because he hated Rodney? Maybe Rodney got in the way. He'd have no hesitation about killing us if he believed we might screw up his plan. Maybe Bozelle was supposed to get the blood money Rodney intended to shell out for Stephen Cross's death."

"I don't like this," Tony said. "We're opening ourselves up for a sniper attack."

I shook my head. "No. He wants to know for certain we have the kids, and at the first good opportunity he'll swoop."

We pushed our way down the block until we got to Broadway. We turned left and then headed uptown toward the TKTS booth, a Times Square institution noted for discount theater tickets. People were already lined two to three deep against the metal police barriers near the site, but we found one small area where Tony and I could squeeze to the front. We had an unobstructed view across Broadway. We placed our fake kids next to our sides and put our hands on top of their heads.

I suddenly felt antsy. "The waiting begins . . . ."

"Yep. Keep our eyes open. Scan the rooftops as well. I doubt he's up there, but you never know."

The hour dragged by in the company of restless parents and children. I heard it all—screaming, laughing, crying, coughing, sneezing, cajoling for roasted peanuts or a stuffed toy to commemorate the parade. The parents were either obsequious or oblivious. After sixty minutes of inane conversation about which balloon or band might be coming down the street, a pet hamster seemed like a much more attractive option than a child. Tony and I kept alert, but we didn't see anything that aroused our suspicions.

Little by little, the parade approached. We heard the applause of those gathered north of us and the distant sound of a marching band. We craned our necks and saw the first of the gigantic balloons floating down the street like bloated tethered birds. The kids around us grew increasingly frantic, flailing their arms and asking their parents to lift them up on their shoulders.

"Do you think we should lift our kids?" Tony asked.

I laughed and thought about it, but decided that was even too crazy for me. "Just keep a hand on each of their heads."

The parade finally reached us, resulting in a general pandemonium in the crowd. I wasn't really interested in what was happening on the route. What interested me was the goings-on in the crowd. A loud marching band from Alabama with twirlers and a color guard had just passed by when Tony tapped my hip with his hand.

"Look," he whispered, trying to talk without moving his lips. "Directly across. A man in a camouflage jacket."

Tony was right. A man with short dark hair weaved through the crowd. He was wearing sunglasses and popped in and out of my vision like a target in a shooting gallery. Every time his head appeared he was looking at us. He ended up under a darkened theater marquee.

"There's one way to find out," I said. "Stay here."

The police didn't like it, but I had noticed people crossing the streets at various times, mostly to take photographs. I hopped over the barrier and was immediately hailed by a cop.

I smiled and shouted, "My wife and kids are across the street."

He scowled, but waved me on.

The man I was after reacted like a hunted deer and disappeared in the throng. I found my way through an opening in the barriers and craned my head. My height was a disadvantage. The crowd against the barrier slowed me down, but eventually I caught sight of the man I wanted. He was running south toward Forty-Fifth at a good clip, then he turned left heading east toward Sixth Avenue. The crowd was thinner there and the cops had less of a presence.

I rounded the corner and yelled, "Bozelle."

He broke his stride and stopped next to a woman who was walking in the same direction with her daughter. He grabbed the girl from behind like a sack of groceries, turned, and held her in front of him. He pulled a pistol out of his coat and held it to her head. The woman screamed and he shouted, "Shut up or she's dead."

I stopped.

"Get back, Harper," he said. "You know what I want."

Sobbing, the woman fell to her knees like a supplicant in church. She reached out with clasped hands toward her child.

Bozelle stepped into a small alley, hidden enough that he could hold the girl without being seen. She was remarkably calm; her eyes were fixated on her mother.

"Let the girl go," I said. "Whatever you want, work it out with me."

"You're a fool," he shouted. "A fucking faggot fool. You have no idea what's happened." He laughed and then pointed his gun toward me. "You hated the bastard, too."

"Let her go," I said. "I'll meet you wherever you want."

He smiled. "That's an opportunity too good to pass up. I'll let you know where. But bring the kids with you."

He disappeared down the alley, clutching the girl against his chest.

I ran to her mother and put my hand over her mouth. "Please, be calm. Stay here and don't say a word. I'll get her back."

I peered into the passageway. It ran between two relatively tall brick buildings and then opened into another larger alley that ran east and west. Bozelle and the girl were gone.

I wished I'd holstered my .357. I crept down the cramped space, dodging electrical outlets and decaying cardboard boxes. It smelled like stale urine and puke, which reminded me of where I'd spent some nights in my New York City hustling days. It wasn't a pleasant memory. I reached the intersection of the two alleys and peered cautiously to my left. I saw nothing but a long corridor, which I assumed opened somewhere near Broadway. Looking right would be riskier. Bozelle could be around the corner and I could end up with a gun in my face—a chance I had to take.

Better my hand than my head. I stuck my left hand out in the space and moved it up and down. Nothing.

I looked around the rough edge of the building and saw two tiny feet connected to two tiny legs in a doorway about twenty-five feet away. I ran to the kid and scooped her up in my arms. Bozelle was gone. She grasped my neck and hung on, sobbing as I took her back to her mother. When I stepped out of the alley, the woman enfolded us in a bear hug. I released the child and she collapsed in her mother's arms.

"I'm going after that man," I said. "Take care of your daughter."

I had already decided not to wait for the police. Their presence around my apartment might be comforting, but I didn't want New York cops getting involved in my business. I knew what Tony would think, but my internal distrust of the police was still strong.

"Thank you for saving her," the woman said, barely catching a breath. She kissed my cheek.

I ran into the alley and this time turned left. It did indeed open into a narrow passageway at Broadway very near the theater marquee where we had first spotted Bozelle. The parade was still going on. I waved at Tony. He spotted me and waved back. I managed to weave my way across the streets and stood huffing next to him. I told him what had happened.

"You didn't wait for the police?" he said. He was giving me another of those, "You're crazy, you've really fucked up" looks. I should have expected it from an ex-cop.

"No. Pardon my French—but they'll fuck things up."

"Yeah, fucking things up by saving our lives and giving us and the kids police protection."

I glared at him. "One thing you have to realize about me is that cops have made my life hell. Their intervention in this case will only prolong the inevitable and probably lead to someone's death. There's no need to get the New York City Police involved."

Tony looked down and whispered under his breath, "I think you've made a big mistake."

"That's the difference between you and me. I take those chances."

He glared back. "Well, I don't." He grabbed his fake child and stormed away.

I yelled after him to come back.

"Don't bother asking," he said. There was more anger in his voice than I'd ever heard.

I grabbed my fake kid and moved through the crowd. "Where are you going?"

"To the garage to get Vicky. I'll be by to get my stuff and then I'm heading over to Ophelia's. I'll find a place to park until she and the kids get home."

"Don't be crazy," I said.

He laughed while his eyes spit fire. "Me? Crazy?" He turned and I heard him say, "Have a nice life."

I put the kid down on the sidewalk and watched as Tony walked away. I was alone again. A sinking feeling hit my stomach and my heart turned over in my chest. I wanted to call out for him, but I couldn't. Maybe it was better this way. Maybe I had a better chance of getting Bozelle than I would if Tony hung around. I picked up the duffel bag kid and felt stupid as I walked back down a crowded Seventh Avenue. Bozelle could have been following me and I couldn't have cared less. Damn. The hardest part of getting emotionally involved with someone was allowing yourself to be vulnerable. I questioned myself and my reasons for falling for Tony. If our relationship continued I would have to adjust the way I cooked, the way I slept, the way I spent my free time. Maybe even change the way I would die. Was it worth it? I wasn't sure as I walked back the few blocks to my now lonely apartment.

Tony barely spoke to me when he picked up his luggage. He was in and out in less than five minutes. I attempted to hide my disappointment and confusion in the guise of getting ready for work at Han's. Tony would be spending the night with Ruthie and John because Ophelia had already made it clear she needed to work Thanksgiving weekend. Club Leo would be open and ready for business at ten p.m.

Norm could tell something was wrong when I arrived at work. "You look like you lost your best friend." He patted my back.

"I did. Tony."

"Ouch. Let's talk when it's closing time."

We did. The evening was busy and there were piles of dishes, pots, and pans to be washed. Why so many people wanted Chinese food on Thanksgiving was beyond me, but Han's was packed. While I was scrubbing, I told Norm the whole story: what was on the tape he gave me, Rodney Jessup's death, who was behind the shooting at the restaurant, my trip to Richmond, and my encounter with the deranged marine at the parade. Norm was fascinated and astounded that I had been involved in the whole Rodney Jessup affair from the beginning.

"It's like I've been working with a celebrity all this time," he said. "Why didn't you tell me?"

"What good would it have done? My checkered history has no relationship to this job. I gave up my bodyguard dreams to be a dishwasher." I looked at him, judging his reaction. "It was a good choice. I thought the Combat Zone murders and Jessup were part of the past—chapters to be forgotten."

"The past is not easy to be rid of," Norm said, and then smiled. "One often has to ride on it, be it a black or white horse."

"Ancient Chinese proverb?"

"No, but the past can come back to haunt you."

"Tell me about it. Today was a prime example. I pissed off Tony because of the way I feel about cops. Maybe he was right. Maybe I am crazy . . . and stupid."

Norm smiled with his whole face; his eyes lit up. "You could always apologize. You're not used to living with someone. God knows I am, with a wife and three kids. Sometimes you have to bend in order not to break."

I scowled and stuck my hands in the dishwater. The warm suds felt slick against my skin and in their own way they were comforting. "Enough platitudes. You've been reading too many fortune cookies."

"Those little printed pieces of paper are just common sense. Try it. You might like it. On the other hand, the lucky numbers suck."

"Thanks for the advice, Ms. Landers, but I have to work this out on my own. In my gut, I feel I did the right thing."

As the hour neared eleven, I closed the restaurant with Norm and the crew. We all went our separate ways. I wanted to run home and call Ophelia's, hoping Tony would pick up the phone, but I thought better of it. He needed time to cool off and I needed time to think. A scarier thought arose in my mind. Carol and Tony's sister were supposed to arrive in New York the next day. There was no way to head them off. I would have to deal with them on my own.

I was careful as I rounded the corner to my apartment, but everything looked calm on the rooftops and sidewalks of Forty-Seventh Street. I was pretty sure Bozelle knew Tony had been hanging out at my apartment and therefore I wasn't as easy a target as he might have wanted me to be.

I walked down the stoop, opened the door, and locked it behind me. I switched on the lights and threw my keys on the couch. My apartment was back to its lonely, cavernous state after days of being vibrant and full of life. I sat down at the kitchen table and lit a cigarette. If I'd had any booze in the house, I would have dragged it out and broken my sobriety. I watched the white smoke drift toward the lightbulb over the kitchen sink. There was no need to sit on it and blow smoke out through the window. Tears stung my eyes. I wiped my cheeks with my free hand.

"Pull yourself together, Cody," I said to the empty room. "Just because your boyfriend left you and a killer wants you dead, doesn't mean you have to get all verklempt." I stubbed out the cigarette and headed for bed, suddenly feeling very drained by the day. "Tomorrow will be another day." I looked at a red dress, very similar to Ophelia's, hanging in my closet. It reminded me of the times I used to hustle in drag, when every action I took was numbed by drugs or alcohol. I was so high I hardly knew up from down. Those days didn't seem so bad now. For the first time, I felt I was losing control of my life to love and it scared the crap out of me.

Love sucked.

CHAPTER
TWELVE

AT THREE A.M. THE PHONE RANG. THE VOICE WAS
rough and phlegm-filled, as if the caller had smoked a pack of
cigarettes within a few hours. I shook my head awake, wondering
who was on the line. It wasn't Tony—it was too late for him to be
awake. The guy's speech was slurred, too. A pack of fags and half
a bottle of booze under his belt.

"You know who I am," he said and then chuckled.

Before I could get a word out, he continued, "And I know who
you are and where you live. But I knew that a long time ago." He
drew out the word "long" to its ultimate length and then stumbled over "time ago." The man was having his own private party.

"Bozelle?"

"None other."

I didn't respond hoping he'd bumble forward giving me some
clue to his whereabouts.

"What's the matter," he said. "Cat got your cock?"

He laughed at his own miserably twisted cliché. I still was
holding out hope that he'd hang himself.

"Or maybe that pretty cop boyfriend of yours is having a late night snack at dick diner. If he can *find* it!"

That pissed me off. No one insults my privates.

"Leave my dick out of this—and he's not my boyfriend. What do you want?"

The line fell silent. When he spoke next he sounded like a sober man with deadly intent.

"I want those kids."

"Why?"

"None of your business."

"You're getting nothing from me, and the kids are going to stay safe until you're in jail."

He breathed in deeply. "Okay, let me put it this way. You hated that bastard as much as I did. I read the papers about the Combat Zone murders. I know you found your faggot friend frozen to a cross. One way or another, Rodney Jessup killed him through his inaction. Well, he also killed something I valued as well."

"Go on."

He exhaled. "That's as far as I go. If you want an explanation, make up your own story. I'm giving you one last chance. Deliver the kids to St. Patrick's Cathedral today at sunset. Most of the tourists should be out of the way by then. Leave them in the pews near the Fifth Avenue entrance while you go up front to pray or whatever the hell you want. Don't turn around for five minutes or they die. If you do as I say, I promise the kids won't get hurt, and I'll get what's coming to me."

"And if I don't?"

"Then your sorry ass is dead. And your pretty boy when I find him, too. I'll kill you both. Rodney couldn't escape—you won't either."

The line clicked and died.

Great. A megalomaniac marine. My head swam and my nerves tingled. I wanted to ask him one last question: "How did you get my number?" I'd asked the same question of Rodney who told me he had his ways. Apparently, Bozelle had his ways, too; my brain was beginning to fit together the pieces of the jigsaw puzzle. And it wasn't a pretty scene.

I tossed and turned until about six and then fell into a fitful sleep until eight. A sickly gray light filtered through the blinds. I jolted awake and felt for Tony, but my bed was empty.

I pulled myself out of the warmth, slipped into my favorite silk slip, and settled on the couch. I stared at the phone and, in my head, dialed Ophelia's number. A conversation with Tony was a must, but somehow my pride was getting in the way. The kids were more important than my stubbornness, however. I picked up the phone and dialed.

Tony answered, sounding as sleepy as I felt.

"I'm calling to apologize for yesterday," I said.

"You take too many chances," Tony said, his voice an angry growl. "You're going to get yourself killed, or worse yet, the kids." He stopped. "I don't want to see you dead." He choked on his words.

I sighed. "Give me one last shot. If things don't work out we'll call in the blue."

Tony didn't have to say anything. I could feel his relief through the phone.

"Bozelle's brought things to a boil, but I don't want you around. It's too dangerous. Whatever you do, don't let the kids out of the house today, keep them in sight at all times. Get hold of Abby and tell her to check Carol in at the Waldorf or some other ritzy hotel. Don't let them come here or go to Ophelia's. Everything will be settled tonight. Despite what Abby or Carol say, follow my instructions. Got it?"

"Cody, tell me what's going on. Now!"

"Just do what I say. Everything's going to be okay."

I heard him shout my name when I hung up the phone, but, at that point, my mind was already racing ahead to sunset because I had to pick out the right dress and makeup for my visit to St. Patrick's.

My door thudded several times during the day, but I didn't answer. I assumed it was Tony, but I didn't want him to know I was at home. I felt pretty certain that Tony was safe from Bozelle. He wouldn't try anything until after his deadline with me had passed. But all hell would break loose after the sun slipped below the horizon.

I called Norm and asked for the day off. He wasn't happy because I'd only worked a few nights since I'd come back from Virginia. But when I told him it was a matter of life and death—and I meant it—he relented. He made me promise to call him as soon as whatever it was I was going through was over. Because of what had happened at the restaurant, I think he was anxious for everything to be over.

I had another call to make—to Janice Carpenter—a necessary conversation if my hunch was correct. I was beginning to put the pieces in place, but I still couldn't be sure.

"For the last time, never contact me again," she said when she picked up the phone. "I don't want to change my number."

"I promise this will be my last call," I said. "But this is important. Just give me one minute." I expected her to hang up, but she stayed on the line. "Tonight, I'm taking Carol's children to St. Patrick's Cathedral. I want to make sure Carol knows this. Maybe she would like to see the kids in church." I didn't give her the exact time for a reason.

Janice huffed into the phone. "Why don't you call her yourself?"

"She's unavailable."

"Those kids have been in church all their lives. I'd be surprised if they *hadn't* been to St. Pat's."

"That's all I wanted to say. You got the message, right—the kids, tonight, at St. Patrick's?"

"I'm not an idiot," she said and hung up.

That was an understatement. I knew Janice Carpenter was no idiot, but I was also aware there was more to her story than I knew. Something bad had happened to set Bozelle off and claim "emotional distress" for a divorce proceeding. Probably only three people in the world knew what that was about: Janice, Bozelle, and the unidentified woman who attended Rodney's funeral. The only other person who might have known about Bozelle's claims about Janice was dead—Rodney Jessup.

I spent the rest of the day plotting my strategy. I had no intention of getting murdered in St. Patrick's. I rooted around in my New York City travel books and found a couple of pictures of the cathedral. I, of course, had never set foot in the place. Its only interest for me would have been architectural. I had passed by it many times and had been impressed by its massive structure, but I had no desire to go inside. I studied the pictures, which showed the entrance, the nave, and the choir. I familiarized myself as best I could with the photos so I'd have some idea of what I'd be getting into.

I thought a lot about who I was dealing with. Bozelle was a loose cannon who wanted Rodney's children more than anything else. He was dangerous and I had no doubt that he'd kill me, and Tony, if he got the chance. The kids were another story. Kidnapping for ransom, I was certain, was his objective. The more I pondered the situation, the more I believed Rodney had caused a dreadful occurrence in Bozelle's life. That was only half the equation. The other half was the money. I was pretty sure Rodney had hired Bozelle to kill Stephen Cross. He was looking to recover half a million dollars that he never got—money he felt he was entitled to. That was about as much as I could surmise.

I clicked on the radio to get the weather report. The sun would be setting about four thirty p.m. If the overcast held, it would be darker earlier at St Patrick's, which lay in the shadow of the tall Rockefeller Center buildings to the west.

My first inclination was to wear the sequined, red dress I loved so much; however, I didn't want to look like a high-priced call girl. Not that there was anything wrong with turning tricks. I'd hustled enough in my younger days. But no self-respecting prostitute would wear red sequins on the street the day after Thanksgiving. Well, maybe Ophelia. And the dress was too flashy for a Mass, which I figured might be on tap for early evening in the cathedral. Bozelle had probably figured that out, too, and picked a time when the least amount of people would be in the church.

I decided on something much more subtle, a gray suit, more like Kim Novak's classic attire in *Vertigo*. However, I wasn't pulling my hair back in a bun like Hitchcock demanded of his star. My blonde wig was going to fall loose and free, like brunette Judy Barton before her makeover into Madeleine. The longer tresses would hide the side view of my face.

The suit needed a light pressing so I dragged out my ironing board. I picked out my wig, a pair of gray suede shoes with moderate heels that matched the suit, and a white scarf for my neck. Fortunately, I also had a long coat that was a perfect match, although the lapels were a little too wide to be in fashion. The coat would have to do. I thought about evening gloves and reconsidered because my fingertips might be too slick to hold onto my gun. Instead, I picked out a pair of functional black ones for the walk across town.

I shaved my chest and started my makeup regimen about two p.m., giving myself a good basecoat on my arms, upper chest, neck, and face. The lip and eye makeup were the most difficult. I wanted something compatible with the gray. I tried a light flesh color, but it was too washed out. A very light pink seemed to work on the lips. I didn't go heavy on the mascara or eyeliner. By three thirty, Desdemona was in full bloom and ready for action. There was something satisfying about getting into character. I liked this other part of myself that didn't have to wash dishes or put up with bullshit. Desdemona was free to wander about the city doing whatever she wanted to do.

I holstered my gun under my shoulder, put on my coat, took a deep breath, and stepped out the door. The crisp air felt good in my lungs after spending the day in the heat of my apartment. Sometimes I could catch the watery smells of the East River over the steamy subway and sewer odors of Midtown. This afternoon was one of those days.

I wondered if Bozelle or Tony might be lurking outside my door, but nothing seemed to be stirring on the block except the usual cast of characters, including Mrs. Lonnigan tramping down the street with her bottle.

I headed east on Forty-Seventh. St. Patrick's was a straight shot across town. I crossed Ninth, Eighth, Broadway, Seventh, Sixth, until I reached Fifth. Then I turned north toward the cathedral. The church, though not diminutive by any means, always seemed an iconoclastic throwback to an earlier time, as if an alien race had set down a mystical building in the middle of New York's stone and glass towers. One couldn't help but be awed by the site of the Gothic Revival architecture and its twin spires stabbing like knives into the evening sky. The lights were coming up around the city and the spotlights on St. Patrick's bathed the structure in a cool gray. I was not a churchgoing man, but there was something magnificent about the cathedral. I could feel its presence, its spiritual fingers grasping for me, before I reached the massive bronze doors.

The huge sculpture of *Atlas*, bearing the weight of the world on his shoulders, was situated directly across the street. The irony was not lost on me. The only thing better would have been to put him in a dress.

I walked up the steps of the church, throwing an extra sway in my behind as I climbed. My skin itched with nerves, but I was used to keeping them under control. I liked being right on the edge, but not out of control. The importance of my task felt monumental; it didn't hurt I was there to bring down a bad guy. A man and woman, tourists I presumed, pushed open the massive doors and I stepped inside the lofty expanse of the cathedral. The sight was overwhelming. The pictures in my travel books had not captured the in-person visual effect. The smell of burning candles wafted to my nose.

Huge fluted columns soared upward like palms, and ended in spidery buttresses spreading like cobwebs across the ceiling. The last vestiges of light seeped through the stained-glass windows, and, despite the failing rays, illuminated saints, rose windows, and glass panels colored in blue, red, and yellow shimmered on the supporting walls. The windows' delicacy gave an airy effect to the immense space. The glass was predominately blue, which now was turning indigo in the sunset.

I looked at my Lady Timex. It was a few minutes before sunset. More tourists than I had anticipated were strolling through the cathedral's aisles. Not good news. I decided to join them and scope out the territory. I took a few steps, turned, and looked back at the massive organ I had just walked under. I continued to the right, past altars and shrines glittering with novena candles. I stopped short of the sanctuary before turning around. An older woman and a younger man, separated by the center aisle, knelt in prayer near the front of the cathedral. My eyes caught sight of the massive marble *Pieta* folded gracefully into a curve of the ambulatory.

Following the flow of the walkway, I looked back toward the entrance. More people were filing out than in, but about fifteen remained inside—more than I was comfortable with. As I watched the doors, two nuns, dressed in full black habits, entered and then knelt at the first altar near the small gift shop. That was my next stop. Bozelle could be hiding among the cards and crucifixes. I only had to walk past it to see that wasn't the case. A stout lady with gray hair standing near the register gave me a smile.

My nerves continued their twitch and I decided to take a seat a few rows from the back in a scuffed brown pew that looked as if it had been there for a hundred years. It probably had. More behinds than I cared to think about had endured Mass on this bench. I slid in on the slick wood, adjusted my dress, and looked down to the High Altar. I kept my eyes open to any sudden movements or any strange figures lurking about, but the cathedral was quiet—one might say in a prayerful, meditative mood. Maybe everyone had eaten too much turkey on Thanksgiving. Nothing unusual was happening. I waited for ten minutes.

Anxiety finally overtook me. My skin crawled. It was easier sitting in the Déjà Vu porn theater in Boston waiting for Chris Spinetti, the crazy cop, to show up than to be in St. Patrick's. At least in the theater, the lights were dim, I knew the place like the back of my hand, and I had a fighting chance against someone trying to jump me. In the cathedral, I felt exposed, vulnerable, and as naked as if I hadn't been wearing my smart gray suit at all. The place gave me the creeps.

To my right, I saw a black habit flowing toward me. I realized too late that a second nun, shorter, was bearing down on me from my left. A pair of rough hands pushed me down the pew. The bigger nun plopped herself beside me and stretched out her long legs. In a flash, I was surrounded by two of the Lord's good emissaries attired in their finest. I quickly got the idea they weren't there to pray—particularly when I felt a pistol barrel, concealed underneath the habit, being pushed against my ribs.

I looked at the nun to my right. A silver crucifix hung glittering down to the waist; a rosary hung from a belted sash.

Bozelle stared back at me, rage gleaming in his eyes.

"Where are the kids, Harper?" he whispered through his teeth.

"A little late for Halloween, aren't we?" I asked.

"I'd watch the smartass comments, *Des*, or your guts will be splattered all over St. Patrick's."

"You know me too well," I said. "How come I don't know much about you?"

He shoved the gun harder against my ribs and I winced. Another weapon poked through the habit on my left side. The woman wearing it had slits for eyes and arching brows. Her face had an outdoor tanned color, and I got the idea that she, regardless of her height, was well muscled. Whatever Bozelle was serving, she was willing to dish it out as well.

"You're pretty easy to pick out in a cathedral," he said. "Are Jessup's brats coming or do I have to kill you now?"

"Did you think I was going to hand them over without reservations—a little something for me?" I thought I'd bluff my hand.

"What do you mean?"

The old lady who had been praying near the front of the church walked toward us. As she approached, Bozelle lowered his head. The woman took a dollar bill out of her purse and dropped it in his lap. "Thank you, Sister, for all you do." She sauntered off behind us.

"See what happens when you serve your maker," I said to him. "Fortune falls into your lap."

"Shut the fuck up," he said.

"I could have taken advantage of that distraction, but I didn't. I want to work with you. You're right. I hated Jessup as much as you did. I want the whole family wiped out."

He turned slowly toward me, his glassy eyes narrowing as they focused on my face. "I don't believe you."

"I can turn over Ruthie, John, and Carol, too. I'm sure she had something to do with all that you've gone through."

"How would you know that?"

176

"All I have to do is read between the lines of the newspaper clippings. Your divorce from Janice must have been messy. Mental cruelty is never fun—unless it's part of the game. Who doesn't like a little S&M now and then?"

"Pervert." Bozelle spit the word out. "You're nothing but a disgusting pervert. That you would even be sitting in this church dressed like a woman fries my ass."

"You're one to talk. I guess God has taken the holiday weekend off. Otherwise, He might have dropped the ceiling on us."

"What do you want?"

"Half the money you were supposed to get." I caught him off guard.

He couldn't believe I knew. I let my gut do the talking.

"Rodney offered you a tidy sum to kill Stephen Cross, the one man who could destroy him. But a small-time neo-Nazi beat you to it. Half a million dollars down the drain. You must have been pissed. Rodney paid me half that to protect him. I did a piss-poor job."

Bozelle laughed, then caught himself, and covered up his glee with a cough. "I almost put a bullet in your head the day I killed Rodney, but I thought you were already dead. I heard a car in the distance. Maybe I had the wrong idea about you . . . go on."

"Not much else to say. You let me go and I deliver Carol and the kids to you tomorrow wherever you want. You get the goods you're after and I get to keep my half of the money. Simple as that."

"I like that idea," he said, "but I need some insurance." He smiled and his teeth glistened. "You're coming with us. Tomorrow you make the call and make good on your promise. We have nice overnight accommodations for a special guest."

I shrugged. "Whatever you say. I'm ready when you are."

Bozelle looked around. The crowd had dwindled to maybe ten or so. I hadn't had a chance to look back to see if anyone else had come in.

"The two sisters will escort you out," he said.

"Aren't you going to introduce me to Sister Silent on my left."

"Later," he said. "When we get outside, we're going to turn right and go to the side of the church. We want to make sure you're not carrying. You're not supposed to pack heat in church anyway." He laughed at his joke.

"One question before we go," I said. "Why did you hate Rodney so much?"

"Too long a story—the bastard killed someone dear to me." Bozelle looked down as if he was trying to hide the pain in his eyes. "Rodney Jessup was an adulterer and he paid the price. I hope he's rotting in hell. Let's go." He grabbed me by the arm and told his female companion to keep her gun aimed at my back. "When we get out of the pew, stand next to him," Bozelle instructed her. "Don't let him make any sudden moves."

I was covered, with no way to get to my gun. I couldn't reach for Bozelle without getting shot in the back. I couldn't push backward into Sister Silent without taking it from Bozelle. He was too fast and I didn't want to mess with a sharpshooter marine. And there was no telling what kind of a crack shot his companion was.

We turned toward the cathedral entrance and my mouth dropped open.

Tony was standing in front of the bronze doors with his gun drawn.

Bozelle saw him too and in a split second he dropped to the floor and fired at my friend. Three quick blasts to the chest from a semiautomatic pistol knocked Tony against the door. He crumpled and fell. Screams erupted in the sanctuary.

Instinctively, I pushed the woman to my right to the floor. She hit the marble with a thud and her gun spurted out from under her habit and circled underneath a pew.

Bozelle was still prone, but his gun had shifted toward me. He must have thought he'd been set up. He was ready to shoot me when a well-placed bullet knocked the gun from his hand. He screamed and withdrew his bleeding hand into the habit. I looked left toward the gift shop from where the shot had been fired. Abby stepped out from behind one of the Gothic pillars. I took out my gun and covered Bozelle. Abby was on top of the woman, cuffing her, before I could get any words out.

My heart boomed in my chest as I looked at Tony. I shouted his name but there was no response. Abby looked concerned as well, but she kept her gun drawn on the woman. A crowd began to gather. A few of the sightseers raised their heads slowly from the pews where they had taken cover. A man and woman opened the doors to the cathedral. She screamed when she nearly tripped over Tony's body. In what seemed like the longest minute I'd ever experienced, I kept my gun aimed at Bozelle. Blood soaked the habit and flowed across the floor. Two NYPD cops, guns drawn, rushed in the door and called for backup. Abby showed her PI ID and shouted instructions. The whole scene played out before me like a bizarre dream.

Nothing mattered to me but Tony. One of the cops took my place and I sprinted toward the door. It was hard to kneel in my dress, but I finally got down and leaned over his face. A small pool of blood had formed behind his head. I yelled his name and his eyes fluttered open.

"Thank god," I said, hardly aware of what I was proclaiming. "Are you all right?"

"My head hurts," he said. "I must have hit it against the doors." He lifted his sweater and showed me the body armor he was wearing.

"Jesus," I said. "You gave me a scare. I thought you were dead."

Tony leaned up on his elbows and I looked at the back of his head. A two-inch cut near the crown was bleeding profusely.

"Here," I said.

I removed the white scarf from my neck and wrapped it around his head. He looked like Carmen Miranda on a very bad day. "Let's get out of here. Cops give me the creeps."

He managed a smile. "I think we'll have some explaining to do before they let us go. The archdiocese probably doesn't think much of shoot-outs in St. Patrick's."

Tony was right.

CHAPTER THIRTEEN

DAMAGE AT ST. PATRICK'S WAS MINIMAL. NO bullets had lodged in the bronze doors because they had been stopped by Tony's vest. The bullet that passed through Bozelle's hand splintered the back of one of the pews, but the repair job would be cosmetic. Not so, his hand. In my humble opinion, Bozelle wouldn't be firing a gun soon.

We were all hustled down to the local precinct office for another round of cop torture. Despite it being smack in the middle of Manhattan, the office seemed much more relaxed than the station in Buena Vista. All a matter of perception, I thought. I felt more at home here than I did in Rodney Jessup's hometown. The cops had a no-bullshit attitude, but also a sense of humor. Maybe they were loaded with turkey and pumpkin pie, too. Anyway, it wasn't as bad as I thought it would be.

Tony, Abby, and I finally finished sometime after midnight. The cops had been nicey-nice all night. They even put a bandage on Tony's head. We were exhausted. When we left the station, I lifted my hand to hail a cab to my apartment.

Tony put his hand on my shoulder. "Where are you going?"

"Home," I said. "I'm ready to collapse."

I meant every word. I was in no mood for confrontation or making up, whichever direction the wind might blow us.

"Might I get a thank-you?" Tony asked.

Abby nodded.

I sighed. "I didn't expect to see you, but I guess I tipped my hand when I called Janice. That was the point—to make sure Bozelle got the message."

"The first thing Janice did was call Carol," Tony said. "Then Carol called my mobile phone and told me you'd be at St. Patrick's with the kids. She was worried sick."

"She shouldn't have been. I would have never taken the kids. You knew that. Janice's line was tapped by Bozelle. I saw a line control device on the desk at his house. He only had to check his tape machine to hear Janice's calls, even from out of state. That's how he knew Carol's every move. Everything she told Janice was picked up by him." I took off my wig. No one on the street even gave a second glance—just another night in NYC. "By the way, where is Carol?"

Tony laughed. "At Ophelia's with the kids. I need to get back there. Ophelia's at work at Club Leo."

"Carol surprised me," Abby said. "She had no intention of going to a hotel. I thought she might freak out knowing Ophelia's story, but I really think she's grateful to us . . . and to you."

I looked down at the pavement dotted with cigarette butts and black spots of dried gum. "Oh, and thanks for getting me out of a jam." I didn't want to sound too grateful, however. "But I was in control of the situation. I was going to make my move once we were outside the cathedral."

"Sure," Tony said, and then massaged my shoulder.

I wanted him to stop—and I didn't want him to stop. His strong hands felt good through the fabric of my ruffled gray suit.

"Well, I don't have any pressing matters to take care of at home, so I guess I could drop in at Ophelia's for a short visit. Just to say hi to Carol."

"Let's go," Tony said, and put his arm around my waist.

We parked the Crown Vic in the neighborhood and buzzed Ophelia's apartment. Tony had neglected to get a key. The sleepy voice that came back over the intercom was Carol's. She buzzed us in. When we arrived, the door was open. Carol was stretched across Ophelia's green couch. I had misjudged her state of mind. She was more drunk than sleepy. The New York City skyline twinkled over her shoulders. She puffed on a cigarette held in one hand while the other held a tumbler of scotch.

"Happy hunting, kids?" Carol smiled and curled her long legs under her torso.

Abby sat next to Carol while Tony and I collapsed in side chairs.

"Stanley Bozelle is now under arrest for the murder of your husband," Tony said. "I figure he's going to squeal like a stuck pig."

"Charming colloquialism," I said. "I always hated it. Cruelty to animals." I motioned to Carol. "Mind if I join you in a smoke?"

Tony gave me the eye. Obviously, we were still out of sync.

Carol tossed me her pack of cigarettes. I really wasn't in the mood for a woman's slim 100s, but I was begging and couldn't be choosy.

I lit up and asked, "Where are your little darlings?"

She took a swig of scotch and said, "In Ophelia's . . . Robert's bed. Whatever the hell he's called." She swallowed another gulp. "He's a nice guy, putting up with my two for all this time. I have to give him credit."

"Honestly, Carol," I said, "we're all nice here. In fact, we're all a damn sight nicer than Rodney ever was, and if you could get past your God-induced church obsession, you'd see that."

Tony shot me another one of his "you're nuts" looks. The scotch fumes must have affected my brain. Whatever sense of decorum I had disappeared in the evening's drama.

Carol's eyes narrowed on me like a pistol sight on a target.

She puffed on her cigarette and said, "I think you underestimate me. I know when someone's done me a favor, and I know how to repay it."

"Did you know Rodney hired Bozelle to kill my friend, Stephen Cross?"

She looked surprisingly nonchalant. "I only knew what Rodney told me, and most of that revolved around the Bible."

I knocked ashes into the palm of my hand. "Still, the whole story doesn't add up. At least not to me. Why would Bozelle and his wife—?"

"Girlfriend," Carol corrected me.

"Why would Bozelle's girlfriend throw a rubber doll and a pig fetus on your lawn? I assume she did both. When we were having our little chat at the cathedral, his eyes lit up when I said I would deliver *you* and the kids to him. Why was he so eager? What was the point?"

Tony shook his head. "You told him that?"

"I was trying to save my life," I said.

Carol shivered. "I don't know why he wanted to get his hands on us. I'm just glad he didn't."

"I think there's someone who does know the reason, besides Bozelle, of course. Janice Carpenter."

Carol snuffed her cigarette out. "I hate to think that. Janice has been a friend of the family and a friend of mine for so many years."

Tony looked at his watch. "God, it's almost two and my head is killing me. Time for bed."

"It's too late to check in to the Waldorf," Carol said. "And I'm not getting the kids up. We'll leave in the morning. When will Ophelia be home?"

"He usually rolls in about six in the morning and heads straight for bed," Tony said, assured by his knowledge of having spent several nights at Ophelia's.

Carol stretched her legs toward Abby. "I'm going to spend the night on the couch."

Tony looked at his sister.

"I'll crawl in bed with the kids," Abby said. "There's room."

Tony looked at me and his eyes were almost dreamy. "That leaves the two of us."

I was not so kind. "The last I knew we weren't speaking to each other."

"I've reconsidered," he said. "It's too crowded here."

"All right, let's go. This dress has suddenly gotten very uncomfortable."

Tony and I said good night, and Abby shut the door behind us.

When we stepped into the elevator Tony said, "What you did tonight was extraordinary—and I love you for it. You saved three lives, maybe more."

I turned toward him and ran my hands over his chest. He had ditched the body armor earlier in Vicky's trunk.

"I think simple admiration would be sufficient."

We crawled into the Crown Vic and made out like highschoolers. It was nearly two when we walked into my apartment. By the time we got into bed we were both too tired to do anything. That was fine by me. I liked feeling his body next to mine. He snored softly and it was like music to my lonely bachelor ears. The sound was comfortable and cozy.

I was in love.

When I showed up for work at Han's on Saturday, Norm's eyes lit up like the Christmas trees that decorated New York. He reminded me of a puppy with a new toy. He bounced around the sink waiting for all the details of my story.

"Come on, Cody," he said. "Tell me. I want to know every-thing."

"Norm, we're busy."

"Aww, they can wait."

How could I argue with the boss? I filled Norm in.

"So, he left?"

"Yes, this morning. He and Abby loaded up the Crown Vic and drove back to Virginia. Carol and the kids are staying on at the Waldorf for a couple of days and then heading back home—in her Mercedes."

"I always wanted a Mercedes," Norm said. "Maybe someday. Too many kids to put through college now." He stood next to the sink and leaned over so he could look at my face.

I was trying to avoid eye contact.

"And how are you taking this separation from your boyfriend? I told you not to let him get away. He's a real looker."

I flicked suds at him. "If I didn't know better, I'd say you have a man crush on Tony."

"Yuck. No. I don't swing that way. I know he's the perfect guy for you, though."

"Really?"

"Really."

That was as far as the conversation went. That night I slouched home and crawled into bed. I was lonely and I hurt in a way I'd never experienced before. Sad and incomplete, if I had to describe it. I didn't like it one bit.

Tony and I talked almost every night over the next few weeks and he was right. Bozelle, under questioning, had squealed like a stuck pig. Tony's cop friend in Buena Vista, who had sent us the newspaper clippings about Bozelle, managed to obtain a verbal summary of the police interview from a New York cop.

Stanley Bozelle went nuts when he found out his wife, Janice

Carpenter, had had an affair with Rodney Jessup. Apparently, Janice was more than a PR wiz and Rodney was more than a benevolent boss. It was beginning to look like Rodney was a certifiable sex addict, willing and able to put his pecker anywhere, anytime.

If that wasn't enough to send Bozelle over the edge, the next revelation did. Janice admitted she had become pregnant by Rodney and aborted the baby; thus, the doll and fetus dumped on the lawn. Bozelle had lost not only his wife but a child as well. Granted the kid wasn't his, but his moral sense was outraged.

Rodney tried to appease the ex-marine by hiring him to kill Stephen Cross. Better to keep him in his camp as a paid friend than let him roam loose as an enemy. Bozelle's moral outrage probably extended to homosexuals as well. However, the chance to get half a million dollars from Rodney and then later kill him was too good to pass up. But that plan was snuffed out by extreme irony. Enter Stephen Cross and Hugh Mather, the Combat Zone Killer. Bozelle was too late, he didn't get a dime, and the threats on Rodney began after the ex-marine figured out what he wanted to do.

I figured Rodney suspected Bozelle was after him, but didn't know for sure. Rodney had made plenty of enemies and the guy was one of many. But Bozelle, unlike a lot of others, had a great motive for killing Rodney. A delicate web had been strung and any strange twist could destroy it. With Stephen gone, he was after the kids for ransom. He'd get the money somehow. By the time he'd perfected his plan, Carol and kids were on the move, spending less time in Virginia. Bozelle's own threatening tactics had worked against him. He had to wait for the perfect time. Patience was not one of his virtues.

Janice, it seemed, was in the clear. Maybe Bozelle harbored some love for his ex-wife. His real target had been Rodney. After all, the pious minister had destroyed his marriage and his emotional ability to have children with the woman he married.

The suspect was now in jail nursing a serious wound to his

right hand. When he finally came to trial, a whole lot of bad news would be spread across the US. Carol and Janice would be in the headlines daily.

It didn't take long for Carol to learn the truth. One late afternoon after finishing some halfhearted Christmas shopping at Macy's, I walked into my apartment to the sound of the phone ringing.

"Keep the money," Carol said. "I know Rodney wired you two hundred fifty grand. You deserve it."

I put my two packages on my kitchen table. "Thanks, Carol, but I wasn't planning on keeping it. There are a lot of unfortunate people who have more use for it than I do." I couldn't believe the words had come out of my mouth. Ophelia came to mind. She still needed a lot of money for her medications.

"Do what you like," she said. "Ruthie and John miss you— and Ophelia. They haven't been the same since their trip to New York. I think they're going to be better people for it. Me, too."

I wasn't sure what to say, so Carol filled in the blanks. "There's a saying: 'God chooses your parents, but you choose your friends.' I know what happened between Rodney and Janice now. We're not on speaking terms anymore. I'd like you to be my friend." She sighed.

I kept listening for the tinkle of ice, but Carol sounded sober.

"Thank you. I'd like that."

She said, "Merry Christmas." The line went dead.

That conversation left me with a touch of melancholy. I put on the Carpenters' Christmas album and when "Merry Christmas Darling" came on, a lump rose in my throat. I picked up the phone and dialed Tony. He answered and all the tension I'd been holding since Rodney had shown up at my apartment came out in a torrent of swearing and tears.

"Sorry," I said after I composed myself. "I feel like a blubbering idiot."

"Don't be sorry," Tony said. He paused and then said, "I've missed you."

"Same here. New York can be a very lonely city."

"I can be there for Christmas if you want."

My heart jumped along with my formerly sagging holiday spirit. "You can? You don't have to work?"

"Even I get a day off. I'll be there Christmas Eve. I can take a taxi in from the airport."

"That would be great," I said and pinched myself.

"I wondered when you'd come around."

I shook my head in wonder at his audacity. "Don't push your luck."

"Merry Christmas, darling," he said and then hung up.

I took off my leather boots, sat on the couch, and put my feet up on my old coffee table. I'd never been much for the holidays because they didn't really matter to me. My old preconceptions were falling away. When Tony arrived on Christmas Eve, I was planning to be dressed in a festive holiday outfit. I had already picked it out: a leather harness, boots, chaps, and a red bow tied around a bountiful package. Tony would have plenty of fun unwrapping his gift.

I was going to make it the best Christmas either one of us had ever had.